The Establishment muttered darkly of invaders, sending in a secret task force (roughly one operator per government) to discover what it was all about.

The people said a beerkeg had landed. (Well, after all, that's pretty much what it looked like.) There were the usual humorous articles in the alert press.

Meanwhile a happy lush, perhaps mistaking the outline of the alien ship for some glorious alcoholic heaven, had boarded the beerkeg.

And it had then left.

No one knew what the hell was going to happen.

And two weeks later, the lid blew . . .

This is an original publication—not a reprint.

# ALIEN ISLAND

T. L. SHERRED

BALLANTINE BOOKS • NEW YORK
An Intext Publisher

First Printing: January, 1970

Cover Painting: Carol Inouye

Printed in the United States of America

BALLANTINE BOOKS, INC.
101 Fifth Avenue, New York, New York 10003

# Chapter One

The traditional way to tell a story is to begin at the beginning, but I wasn't there at the beginning.

At that important time I was night barkeep at the only bread-booze-beer stop in Greenbush, population sixty plus, two hundred miles north of Detroit. Three days a week I worked in the cafeteria at Wurtsmith SAC Airbase just outside of Oscoda, ten miles south and just off Lake Huron; all in all a pretty good cover, inasmuch as I'm a native Michigander familiar with the general shoreline from Omer up to Alpena.

On this particular Sunday one of my late regulars stopped for his hamburger and beer midway through his Cheboygan run on US 23. He had Monday morning's *Free Press*, which he usually picked up for me at his terminal before he left Detroit, and while he chomped away on his sandwich I took it over to the pool table where the light was better.

"How about that spaceship?" he said around his bun. I looked up, and he said, "Next page, just inside the headline," and I turned to page three to grin at the subhead—FLYING SAUCERS OR FLYING GLASSES?—and went on to read the short one-column feature.

Rushing the season somewhat, a flying saucer landed Sunday afternoon on Detroit's far east side shortly after the bars opened at noon; at least that was the solid consensus of the customers of the Triangle Bar.

It seems the flying saucer, which was an aluminum beerkeg, landed at a gas station across the street from the Triangle Bar. One of the customers, confessing he just stopped in to change a ten on his way to church, first spotted it and reluctantly decided it was real. The flying beerkeg was instantly surrounded by thirsty denizens of the Triangle Bar, and according to several positive witnesses, it opened up long enough to admit one of the latecomers, tentatively identified as "Hank the Tank."

An anonymous skeptic called police, but before police arrived in their ground-bound vehicles, the flying beerkeg had soared off, silently and straight up, bearing away the presumably happy Hank the Tank. Unfortunately, when this reporter talked to Triangle Bar customers late Sunday afternoon, Hank the Tank (who refused to supply his full name) came in the back door, claiming he had slept all night in his car, and what was all the fuss about?

Stains on Smitty's gas station driveway seemed remarkably like engine oil, and when this reporter left the Triangle Bar it was generally agreed that an aluminum beerkeg (30 feet long? 100 feet long?) full of beer at 25¢ per glass would be a very good thing to have around.

This was Sunday.

Monday afternoon the *Detroit News* had almost the same story, not quite so heavy-humored, with photos of the Triangle Bar, Smitty's Super Service, and assorted people pointing solemnly either at the sky or at Smitty's driveway. Monday evening in Detroit, of course, the lid blew off, and some of the steam seeped two hundred miles north to Greenbush.

Just after bar closing time, the telephone rang when I was dropping the ashtrays in the wash tank.

Mac said, "You used to live on the east side."

"Detroit?" I said. "Twenty years, off and on."

"Do you know where Harper and Chandler Park Drive is?"

I laughed. "The Triangle Bar and Smitty's Super Service and the flying beerkeg? I read the papers, if that's what you mean."

"Do they know you at the Triangle Bar? Have you ever been in there?"

"No," to both questions, I said.

"See me here at nine sharp"—which meant an hour earlier—and he hung up.

While I finished cleaning up for the day bartender (he did, after all, load the bottle coolers for me), I thought about Mac's call. It had to be a positive contact for him to pull me away from almost the end of my search for the noncom who had been peddling photographs of delicate parts of the SAC base. And, whaddya know, my knowledge of Detroit was going to be valuable. I covered my sudden absence with a note to the owner of the bar, left another at my motel (winter rates), and, with a third stuck in the door of the cafeteria-caterer when I drove through Oscoda at four in the morning, headed south.

Mac's office is like any employment agency on Woodward, maybe a little crummier because it's open twenty-four hours for the Skid Row rumdums. Jimbo was at the outer desk reading his lawbook and he gave me the stare that told me Mac was waiting and I was late again. Inside, Mac was rewinding a tape recorder. He hates people who are late. I sat down and watched the reels spin on the machine. He put it on playback, said sourly, "Make yourself comfortable," and started the recorder, and I jumped when I heard a fusillade of shots.

He stopped the machine and raised his eyebrows. "Nerves? Late movie," he said, and looked at his calendar pad. "Channel Two, last night, Monday, eleven-fifty-three P.M." He flipped the switch again; more shots and the standard comment about crooked varmints. Then the volume came up, completely overriding the midnight movie sound track: "Calling Channel Two. Calling Channel Two. Calling Channel Two." A male voice, husky and thick. Mac turned off the recorder. "Nine minutes of this, until someone at the transmitter woke up." He switched it on and the reels spun again. The film noises broke off and another voice came in.

"This is Channel Two. Get off this frequency!" It did not have the sheer strength of the first caller, and the message was repeated several times before it was noticed.

"It's about time." The loud voice broke in again. "That movie is lousy enough to put anybody to sleep."

The voice from the transmitter was furious. "You're on an assigned frequency. This is a federal offense. Now get off the air!"

Although he must have heard it before, Mac ducked his head nervously when the high-powered voice suggested something anatomically difficult. "And shut up for a minute, hey? Just pass the word I'm all right and don't do any shooting."

The voice from Channel Two was incoherent by now. "You're drunk! Get off the air! This is a federal offense." Mac killed the recorder.

"The language gets a little rough," he said.

"So?" I took one of his cigarettes as he put the machine away and went around to his desk chair.

"So it lasted long enough to get a fix on it. Several fixes: one from Selfridge, one from Wurtsmith, one from Wright-Patterson—and one from Omaha."

"Omaha!" I sat straight up.

Mac knew what I was thinking. TV frequencies are line-of-sight. He nodded. "Location, Detroit, plus or minus a few feet. Altitude, sixty-three point seven miles, give or take a few feet. Power—God knows. Enough to blanket twenty states. And nothing on radar. Nothing at all." He picked up an envelope from his desktop and toyed with the flap. "You read the ha-ha funny reports in the papers," and I nodded. "They didn't say that a busload of Boy Scouts on their way to Cobo Hall were waiting for the Harper traffic light. Most of them had cameras and a couple were Polaroids." He reached over with the envelope.

It did look like a beerkeg, but also like a can of beans without the end flanges, almost a perfect shiny cylinder lying on its side with the bottom flattened out. As I leafed through the several Polaroid shots I found it difficult to judge its size, even though it was surrounded by people in various degrees of dress—probably the Triangle Bar customers. There it sat, stolid, strange, not a visible rivet, weld, or marking.

Mac took back the envelope. "No overall shots, but allowing average heights for the gawkers it's close to twenty-five feet in diameter and at least fifty feet long." He dropped the envelope on his desk and leaned back. His chair squeaked.

"How did you get the pictures?"

"The newspaper story. The parents of one of the Boy Scouts got sore and called up the *Free Press*. Our man there"—I hadn't known we had one—"tipped us off and we got there first." He was frowning as he talked. "Some of those pictures were already on the way to photolabs all the way from Rochester to Chicago." He stopped and turned his chair to look out the window at the alley.

I was expected to say something. "How long can you hold the lid on?" This was going to be tougher than the landing in West Virginia, where there had been only three witnesses and a tri-county newspaper to handle.

He did not answer quickly. Then, turning back to face me, "Today, maybe tomorrow. The newspapers are cooperating, but too many people saw it happen this time. Then this break-in on television last night ..." Mac pretended disgust. Out of the entire country this had to happen in his territory. Upstairs the teletypes would be chattering; scramblers purring from Army, Air, Washington. Troubles. Mac came up with a lopsided grin.

"It had to happen some time, didn't it?" Then he got down to business. "We've checked the Triangle Bar. We know the cylinder picked up somebody—at least five witnesses swear it was this Hank the Tank, who walked in—or walked aboard—of his own volition. But Hank the Tank was sleeping in his car, and we hear megawatts pushing a man's voice from sixty miles up. So who is it?"

"Doak the Soak?"

"Funny," he said without heat. "Highly comic. Go get drunk in the Triangle Bar. Get your oil changed at Smitty's gas station. Either it's some customer at the Triangle Bar or it isn't. Find out which. Nobody's reported missing as yet, so he might be a single man. Bachelors are boozers, so go find out, fastest."

I stood up. "I hear, tuan. Go get drunk at the Triangle Bar," and I left.

The Triangle Bar was a big barn: noisy, crowded, dowdy at the edges but mostly clean; and the bartender-owner was a plumpish bustling middle-aged frau with pink curlers in her hair. I found a vacant stool, got my drink, and listened. I listened for two hours. This Triangle Bar was quite a joint.

Everyone knew everyone else: where they were last night, where they worked, their wives or their husbands, their bowling averages. No one paid much attention to me, which surprised me a little. The flying beerkeg—they seemed to think the name was perfect—of course came up over and over again. Eventually the conversation widened enough to include me so I could insert "Is that so?" and "You don't say?" and all the other substitutes for language. Oddly enough, no one seemed to resent even slightly the snide newspaper story, and it got to the point where I could ask why Hank the Tank had been thought to be beerkeg-aviating. Someone said, "Well, it sure *looked* like him," and from then on I heard just how enraged Hank the Tank had been when the newspaper said he wouldn't give his last name. The barmaid quivered gently topside as she explained, "Hank told him, but the newspaper man couldn't even pronounce it, let alone spell it," and she checked the clock. "He's overdue right now for his lunch. Wait until somebody asks him what his name is."

Hank the Tank did show up shortly afterward and he was still smoldering, not only because of the newspaper story but because someone had swung with his new fur jacket. The owner told him to shut his trap and drink his lunch, that there were plenty of sots in her place but no thieves, and that, furthermore, on Saturday night he had sold his fur jacket (which was a long way from being new) to— And she stopped in midstride.

A surprised look spread across her face under the pink plastic curlers. "You sold it to Ken. No wonder we thought it was you that went in the beerkeg!" There was an instant yelp of agreement.

"Ken who?"

"Ken Jordan," said the owner, and when she got a blank stare, added, "Ken the Card Shark," and for the inquirer it was data enough. But not for me, and I had to pry around for another half-hour before I could call Mac at the office.

"Hank the Tank is definitely not in the flying beer-keg," I told him. "He sold his badge of office—a ratty fur jacket—to one Ken the Card Shark. The name is Ken Jordan. About five-ten, one-eighty to one-ninety, sallow complexion, brown hair, and he probably needs a haircut, age between forty and sixty—you heard me, somewhere between forty and sixty. A normal loudmouth but quieter with every drink until he falls off the barstool. Cashes weekly brown bond-paper paychecks from a small toolshop on Hoover just north of Nine Mile Road." I listened to Mac for a minute.

"I don't think so," I told him thoughtfully. "No visible scars, no distinguishing characteristics outside of a permanent thirst and a yen to play any card game any time for dollars or drinks. Ken the Card Shark, remember? Not married, no relatives that he's talked about, lives alone in a room within walking distance of the Triangle Bar. No car; sold it a year ago when they took away his license. He was probably slugged to the ears when he walked into the beerkeg—well, that's what they call it here and they've got me doing it—because the owner doesn't sell booze on Sunday, she says, and Ken the Card Shark buys a fifth and a pint every Saturday to last him over the Sabbath. Now can I get some sleep?"

I waited until Mac checked Jimbo in on my call, which he'd taped, and when he came back on the phone he said, "All right. How long have you covered yourself for up north at Wurtsmith?"

"A few days. Sickness in the family."

"Good," he said briskly. "There's no immediate reason why you shouldn't go back, any more than I brought you down. Just my hunch. Better stick around the rest of the week; two-hour calls when you're not home," and after I hung up the telephone I headed for the upper-income I hadn't seen for almost two months. It took me an hour to rearrange enough dust so that I could flop into bed with a reasonably clear conscience. About midnight I got up, opened a can of soup, and went back to sleep until the telephone rang steadily enough to wake me up. Through the blinds I could see the sun glittering off the snow.

"Just checking," he said. "Planning on anything today?"

"Jimbo," I said, "you didn't call me to find that out. Now what's up?"

He laughed. "Mac's up, and so's the balloon. Just stick around, and if you want to see the elephant just turn on your TV set."

"Channel Two?"

Jimbo had a dirty laugh. "Yeah. Channel Two. Or seven or nine or fifty or anything. Compliments of the management."

I told him to go bag it and on the way to the coffeepot I flipped the TV switch. When I came back into the bedroom there was some imbecilic program in progress and I checked around the dial: quiz games, movies, commercials, and more quiz games. I was wondering why Jimbo had called me when the TV volume roared up.

"Calling the United Nations. Calling the United Nations. Ken Jordan in the spaceship KAYTA calling the United Nations. Calling the United Nations. Ken

Jordan in the spaceship KAYTA calling the United Nations."

The picture was still coming through, although the volume of the call was overriding the sound. I put the coffee cup and the toast down on the nightstand and flicked the band selector; every band, even the dead channels, were blaring forth the call for the United Nations. I reached for the phone and dialed Jimbo at the office. "How long has this been going on?"

He didn't know exactly. At least the last hour. The voice kept breaking in every few minutes.

"I think I'd better come in," I said. "An hour, maybe less," and I shut off the TV set and headed for the shower. As I soaped myself I could not help but wonder why the flying saucers—beerkegs?—had finally decided to identify themselves. We had known, of course, that somewhere, some time it would happen, but we had tried to determine that it would be at a time or place where we could control the issue. There was no doubt in Mac's mind that there *had* been some efforts at communication, or at least recognition. But so far we had managed to keep things under the rug just as had as our opposite numbers in the U.S.S.R., although we had had a lot more difficulty in dragooning our quote free press unquote. We could only hope, when the day came, and it was now here, that the aliens would be friendly; that was not to be counted on, however, inasmuch as we had heard through Moscow that the Kwantung Chinese had zeroed in on one UFO with a battery of postwar 88s. And they had not even scratched the paint—paint?—at point-blank range.

And why had they abruptly decided—and who were "they"?—to land in daylight in a big city? Was it good or bad that a spot had been picked near a bar where some alcoholic was just sodden enough to walk into the invitingly open door or hatch or whatever it was called? In West Virginia, and in North Dakota and in Oklahoma, no one who saw the beerkeg had been silly enough to get close to it. Sensibly, everyone had left immediately for other areas instead of sticking around for the party. And why, why, were they at last showing a pat hand? Naturally we had not discounted the possibility that there were and had been ... well, observers on earth. It would be routine investigation to trace this Ken the Card Shark. But if he were a plant it would mean that "they" were either beings identical with us (and also far beyond us in technology) or unlike us (and still ahead in technology, with the ability to provide perfect cover for an alien plant). Either way, Mac and Jimbo and myself and some others were now out of a job. Not that I cared, but in our group we got a good deal of freedom, much more than the average GS-9 stooge, and it was going to be hard to go back to putting numbers on a piece of paper. The mirror told me before I left that missing a night's sleep had not improved my appearance one bit.

## Chapter Two

It might be of interest to tell how it looked to us at the time.

After Jordan had been calling for two hours, his throat and his patience began to fray in equal proportions. These two hours, and many hours before that, had been hell for Mac, his crew, and his bosses; the fact that there had been a positive contact went right to Washington to The Man and back again, and overseas and back again. Previously there had always been time to whitewash or to cover, but now the dog had found the bone and the neighbors knew it. And when the Jordan voice—still from 63.7 miles up—roared in all over the dial, asking not for The Man or any of his minions but for the United Nations ... well, two hours is not really a long time. The networks could come up with nothing better to do than to supply the usual pablum, and the local channels, with no guidance from God, loyally relayed the network junk because no one dared stick his neck out far enough to admit the Roman candle was up. And so they stirred their sorghum while the switchboards clogged and the newspapers were flooded with calls, until some time in the afternoon The Man decided that the buck *did* stop at his desk. By this time, naturally, everyone within reach of a telephone knew what was going on.

On the grounds that he—Jordan—had originally called on Channel Two's frequency, The Man broadcast straight from his office and his message went out over Channel Two. To give him credit, he spoke himself, announced himself, and repeated it over and over until his own voice grew ragged at the edges. By this time I and Mac and Jimbo were sitting together in the office drinking whiskey and coffee out of paper cups. The Man called again and again, and it was with a marked feeling of relief that we finally heard the familiar detestable voice of Jordan.

"Well, hi, Mr. President," he said, and his voice was unawed and brash. "I was beginning to wonder if anybody was gonna answer. Can you get me somebody to talk to at the United Nations?"

The Man was nylon-smooth. "Well, thank you, Mr. ... Jordan, isn't it? Of course, the United States is a member of the United Nations, and since you're a citizen of the United States you must realize that all contacts with ... with anyone must go through the usual accredited channels. . . . You did say the spaceship KAYDA, didn't you, Mr. Jordan?"

Jordan said, "That's right, but you should say KAYTA, not KAYDA. Hold on just a minute, will you?"

Mac looked at me and we both smiled grimly at the effrontery of a drunk telling the President of the United States to hold the phone.

Jordan came back in. "Jeez, I'm sorry, Mr. President. But they don't want to talk to anyone in any separate government. I told them that we had a sort of a world council of nations here, and they won't deal with anyone else."

The Man coughed solemnly. "You said 'they,' Mr. Jordan. What do you mean by 'they'?"

Jordan said in a tone of surprise, "Why, the people that picked me up. The people here in the ship."

The President pounced. "You said 'people,' Mr. Jordan. Do you mean people just like us?"

There was a short pause, and then this imbecilic Jordan actually giggled. He said, "Well, not exactly, Mr. President. No, they're not exactly just like us. Not by a damn sight. Wait just a minute, will ya?"

The President said sharply, "Mr. Jordan. Mr. Jordan. Mr. Jordan!"

Jordan said, "Sorry to hold you up. What was that you said?"

The President asked, "How do you know they want to talk to the United Nations?"

Jordan's voice was puzzled. "Why, they told me. Oh, I see what you mean. They don't speak American. They taught me their language. That must have been last night."

The President said tightly, "And they taught you their language in one night. How?"

Jordan was cheerful. "Damned if I know. I passed out, and—pow! And I knew what they were saying. Hold on just a minute, hey?"

"Why," said the President, "do you keep telling me to hold on?"

His voice was petulant, naturally; he had been in office for five years and Presidents don't usually wait for anyone except voters.

Jordan was reasonable. "They want to know who's talking and what I'm telling you, and they want to know when they're going to talk to the United Nations. When can I talk to somebody at the United Nations?"

The Man has always prided himself on his public

reputation for making quick decisions. Maybe it was better that way, as it took responsibility from his shoulders and clunked it down somewhere else. He said, "Mr. Jordan, as you know, I'm in Washington. But you can rest assured that in two hours, or less if I can arrange it, you will be in contact with the United Nations, or a spokesman thereof. In two hours or less!"

There was a pause, then Jordan inquired sheepishly, "What time is it, Mr. President? I haven't got a watch. . . . Hold on just a minute." Then he came back. "I don't know how long two hours is, Mr. President; the clocks up here don't work right."

The President sighed. He was licked. "Mr. Jordan," and he hesitated. "Mr. Jordan, can you stay just where you are, and can you stay tuned to this . . . frequency, I believe they call it?"

Jordan was jaunty. "I ain't going noplace. And I don't know how they do it, but I hear you even if I don't see any pictures. But I should know about how long two hours is and I'll be around. You're gonna get somebody from the United Nations for sure?"

The President's tone was bitter but confident. "The United Nations. Two hours, Mr. Jordan."

"OK, Mr. President. Hold it a minute, will you?" He came back with a comment that was requoted later on with glee. "They're very pleased to meet you. That's what the captain told me to say," and then the enormous carrier wave cut out; the picture tube lost the jagged patterns we had been seeing and reverted to its blank gray. We just sat and looked at each other for a long moment, and an announcer's jittery voice returned us to the program that should have been in progress; not even a pause for a news bulletin. As if we needed one.

Mac got up and turned off the set and sat back

down again. Jimbo went out, to come back with the coffeepot; he threw out what we hadn't touched and repoured. He sounded almost happy when he said, "Well, that was the curtain. How much are tickets for the balcony?"

Mac drank his coffee without sugar in two swallows and made a face. "There goes the curtain, all right. But is it coming up or going down?" He put down his paper cup and tried to balance it on the edge of the ashtray. "Damn it, why did it have to happen in a big city? Why didn't they stick to the backwoods, the hills?"

I didn't know. "Why didn't they try a city in the first place? If I wanted to meet somebody I'd certainly go where the crowds were. Why not land in a city the very first thing? Why have they been trying to stay out of sight?"

Mac shook his head. "We've been all through that. Maybe they're afraid; maybe cautious. . . . Well, that's it, I guess. They made *the* first contact. They made it when and where they wanted . . . on their own schedule."

I said, "And 'they.' Who are 'they'?"

Mac gave up trying to balance his paper cup and dropped it in his wastebasket, carefully smashing the ashtray. " 'They'! We know who 'they' are. 'They' are one hell of a long way ahead of us. 'They' have probably been watching us for a lot longer than we may know. 'They' might not even have two legs and two arms and one head. 'They' may be—probably are—smart enough to be able to grind us like a jellybean . . . and may just want to. What else do you want to know?"

Very reasonably, I thought, I asked, "What do we do now? Or, to be exact, what do I do now?"

Mac glared at me and at Jimbo. Then he pulled

himself up out of the rage he had been working himself into. "Yeah. How's the setup at Wurtsmith?"

I admitted that as yet we had nothing definite to go on, nothing that would stand up at a court-martial. "How about annual leave? I'm clear at Oscoda."

He thought it over a minute, then nodded. "All right. Keep in touch."

As I got up and turned to leave I asked, "Out of line to ask what's going to happen?" and I waved my hand at the room around us. The employment-agency front and the upstairs had been there for years, as I understood it, with people like Mac and Jimbo and myself moving in and out as situations changed.

Mac shrugged. "Someone will be here. Not me, I'm afraid." He turned to Jimbo. "Your turn at the Triangle Bar. Take someone if you have to—wipe that silly grin off your face, because anything over twenty dollars comes out of your own pocket—and find out what you can about this Ken the Card Shark Jordan. Stay away from routine; get his habits, his schedules, what he . . ."

I eased out before he could think of something for me to do. Beyond the railing in the outer office were two of the usual drifters, good only for bill-passing, paid by the day, and although their eyes lit up when they saw me I waved to indicate that the bossman would be right out.

I stopped at my desk, picked up a bottle of good whiskey I'd been saving, and took it home with me. I sat drinking it with not too much soda, deliberately staying away from the TV, even from music on FM, hearing not a sound in my apartment outside of the dimly audible personalities of the people downstairs. I didn't want anything except to sleep, because I was scared and I didn't know why.

Ever since I'd been transferred to Mac's group I'd

been chasing UFOs all over the eastern half of the country; we always tried to get somewhere, anywhere, first—but were always getting somewhere, anywhere, too late. And then our questioning, our poking fun, the pressure we'd applied from the top, our gospel-tract sermons—the world-isn't-ready-for-this-yet—released to the intelligent ones who wrote or edited small weekly newspapers (all that we had needed to buck so far—until today), the tame psychiatrists and doctors we'd sometimes used, and the rare out-and-out threats. But now . . . our British friends would say that the gaff was blown. Me, I'd say that we were in the soup. That was the last thing I can remember thinking when I fumbled into bed: we were in the soup. The whole world.

In the morning I felt so surprisingly good that it took very little effort to keep the world out. I didn't turn on the TV until well after the coffee had taken hold. I should have known better, because every program on every channel was clamoring with such a confusion of bulletins that it took very little time to confuse me even more. I gave up, turned off the set after a glance at the clock, and although—with the sense of urgency back in full charge of my mind—it was a physical effort, I spent the next fifteen minutes washing dishes. I turned the set back on just at ten, the regular news broadcast. The announcer looked the way I felt, and I listened hard.

It was true. It was no dream. While I was quietly getting sodden, the President had acted. One John Wesley Ngambi, Interim Secretary of the United Nations, had spoken with Ken the Card Shark, 63.7 miles up, late the previous evening. Ken the Card Shark had informed Ngambi that he had been asked to notify the United Nations that one Captain Lee of the cruiser KAYTA would like to visit his organization to establish communications, and would tomorrow be all right? This Ngambi (they showed him speaking, in a taped insert in a corner of the picture) was made of strong stuff. His face, so black it seemed blue, showed only polite interest.

"Of course," he said with real courtesy. "At the captain's convenience. Where and when would the captain suggest?"

The alcohol-brusk voice of Ken the Card Shark—let's call him by his right name, Ken Jordan, although it was a long time before I could forget the Card Shark part—came in rough and loud. He said, "Hold on a minute," and there was a short pause during which Ngambi's expression was expectant and calm. Jordan came back on. "How about tomorrow?"

Ngambi nodded pleasantly. "Of course. May I ask"—and now his composure juddered a bit—"where? And when?"

Jordan's disembodied voice said, "The United Nations building—the big one with all the windows. I saw pictures of it. I can find it. Hold on a minute." Another pause. "I just pointed it out to the captain on the screen."

*On the screen,* I thought to myself. I'd flown many times over New York at forty thousand feet and had had a hard time picking out the city, and Jordan was at 63.7 miles. *On the screen.*

Jordan went on, "All right, we'll be there tomorrow about ... about ... wait a minute," and again the Alice-in-Wonderland pause, while I visualized a shark shuffling a euchre deck and conversing with a misshapen blob behind a stack of blue chips.

Jordan said, "When the sun is directly over this United Nations building, straight up. I haven't got a watch," he added almost wistfully. "Wait a minute—"

and I felt like heaving a rock at Ngambi's image, which had opened its mouth to start to reply.

"We'll land right in front of the building, if it's all right with you," politely.

This was getting to Ngambi. He looked around and rubbed his forehead. "If it's all right with me. . . . Of course, Mr. Jordan. When the sun is directly over the United Nations building. When the sun is directly overhead." He made it sound perfectly sane—a spaceship landing in the front yard at high noon. Tea and trumpets.

Jordan said, "I didn't get your name the first time." A pause. "Would you spell it so I can get it right?"

"John Wesley Ngambi," and he spelled it letter by letter.

"Ngambi?" I could imagine Jordan staring down at the odd consonants.

Firmly: "Ngambi!" There is nothing that irritates a man with a foreign-sounding name like being made to acknowledge it, and Ngambi showed his irritation. But it seemed to do him good, startling him out of his urbanity. "Mr. Jordan, you must admit that this is . . . this is a rather momentous and rather . . . peculiar occasion. Before this meeting tomorrow, would you find it possible to supply a bit more background information?" The Oxford accent was never stronger.

Jordan's voice was flat Midwestern. "Sure, Mr. Ngambi," and he struggled with the *ng* sound.

The secretary picked his words very carefully. "Are you interpreting, Mr. Jordan? I understand that overnight you have learned a completely foreign language. This, in itself, is quite beyond comprehension."

Jordan grunted. "I can't figure it out either. You know what happened? I guess I walked into this thing—thought it was a— No, honest, I just had a snootful and it seemed like a good idea. The next thing I knew I was laid out, and I woke up with the damnedest hangover I ever had in my life." I could visualize him rubbing his head. "They cured the hangover in a couple of minutes," he added happily.

Ngambi took a deep breath. "Exactly, Mr. Jordan. And may I ask, who are 'they'? You say you are going to land a spaceship which is far beyond anyone's capabilities—and beyond belief for most of us—in a few hours from now. Who, sir, are 'they'? What is this cruiser KAYTA? Who is this Captain Lee?" His veneer was cracking; questions had started spilling out, and he caught himself.

Again Jordan left the air dead. I bit my nails while I waited for his answer. "Mr. Ngambi," he finally came back to say, "when I ask them where they come from I can't understand what they say. The captain says some kind of a map I don't know the word for would show it. The captain doesn't think it's very important."

"Not important," Ngambi breathed. "Possibly. One more question, Mr. Jordan. Captain Lee: what is Captain Lee like?"

There was a long silence, and when Jordan spoke again even his raspy voice was changed, tighter, more careful. "Captain Lee," he said slowly. "Captain Lee. You wouldn't believe me, Mr. Ngambi; you wouldn't believe me. You'll have to see for yourself. So long, Mr. Ngambi," and the relayed hum of the carrier wave ceased. Ngambi's inset in the corner of the tube flicked out as the news broadcaster came back on the screen.

"And this astonishing series of events is now coming to a head," he said professionally. "Within ninety minutes, at twelve noon, Eastern Daylight Saving time, it is expected that the unknown cruiser KAYTA, with its mysterious Captain Lee—emissary of a new, strange, and certainly alien civilization—will appear on the actual doorstep of the now even more vitally important United Nations. In a moment we will hear from Sir Henry Laski, internationally known scientist, concerning the incredible happenings of barely the last twenty-four hours. But first, a word from your local appliance—"

I reached over and killed the set, sat there looking at the clock that was circling its hands toward the time an hour and a half away when man would hear from—who? Another planet? Or would it be from . . . I pulled my mind away, and to hell with it. But whatever was going to happen, I thought, I was going to have some company; I wasn't going to be alone. After I made a stop in the bathroom I was going to find myself a crowded saloon with a TV set, and if I felt like getting slugged I'd have another barkeep's shoulder to cry on.

I should have known better. The light traffic on the streets should have warned me, with apparently everyone home listening and watching their own sets. Families huddled together, waiting for the strangeness that was to come. Me, the only customer, and a bartender (obviously rather glad to have someone for company) watched the cruiser KAYTA come in.

# Chapter Three

The longer telephotos picked it up high in the air before the crowds around the United Nations Plaza, held back by police, could see it. With lenses aiming almost directly at the sun, the reflections shooting off like darts of fire made it impossible to see anything clearly until the photographers switched to different camera angles. So we had it dimly in sight long seconds before the audio carried the excited whistles and yells and shouts and screams of the waiting mob as they spotted it.

It came straight down, neither fast nor slow, no hovering or sideslip or hesitation, directly and purposefully. Over the din of the crowd, the announcer's voice was unheard—and unnecessary, because the spaceship spoke for itself. It came down, down, never hesitating until it became plainly visible to the most myopic eye. There were gasps as for a moment it seemed as though it wasn't going to stop, but then, maybe twenty feet from the pavement, it slowed to a taxi stop—as though it were calculating—and simply dropped the last few feet and came to rest. It rested not like an elevator, with cables stretching or recoiling, not like a helicopter, its rotors drooping or shock absorbers bouncing—it just rested.

After the first few seconds it was obvious no one was going to get within yards, and the camera stared steadily at the ship. It was gray. Not silver gray, not aluminum gray, not battleship gray, just gray. And it *was* like a beerkeg lying on its side, with the bottom slightly flattened so that it wouldn't roll. No seams, no rivets, no paint, no ornament, no holes, no protrusions. It just rested there. If it had been black it would have been menacing.

Several minutes elapsed while the *staatspolizei* herded the rabble back behind their ropes, and still it rested there. The noise from the crowd died down, the police eased off on their hold-back wrestling now they'd won the battle, and the voice of the TV announcer at last became audible. What he was saying seemed so unimportant that at last even he ceased trying; everything fell quiet. And still it rested.

Then there was a quick flash of light as a great section of the hull, hinged where it joined the ship at the bottom, dropped out and over and fell to the pavement, forming a gangplank to the inside. I noted automatically that nothing bounced or quivered, but I was trying to see inside the thing as the camera belatedly zoomed in for a closeup through the now open . . . doorway? But the sun was directly overhead and nothing inside could be seen, and the tension in the crowd was as scary as the silence. Then, anticlimax.

Ken Jordan walked down the slanting metal. No alien could be so absurdly crumbummish, with his work shirt open at the collar, faded unpressed work pants, and the ratty secondhand jacket bought from Hank the Tank a million years ago. Jordan stopped at the end of the metal plank, rubbing his eyes in the bright sun, and he shied widely when a spontaneous salvo of disorganized yays slammed his ears. Startled, he realized the cheering was for him and almost preened himself, before he seemed to realize what he looked like and at once appeared embarrassed. What a representative of Earth to be an interpreter, or anything else! He was your maudlin, friendly neighborhood barfly, now sober and ugly. The spasmodic cries of "Yay!" and "Hey!" died down, and I think he was thankful; then he turned back to face the gap in the hull and it was plain that he was telling someone—or something—that everything was all right, and that he was waiting. And so was everyone else waiting, the world, and the bartender in our dim and silent bar, and me.

Then there was a flicker of movement, and we saw it.

It was gray, dull gray. Human-size, yes, but gray and beastly. Its head was no head; it was solid, globular, and expressionless. Its body slid, glided out into the bright sunlight, visible now to the stunned-silent crowd. The body had no tentacles, but some sort of camouflage wrapped the whole form—of which nothing whatever could be seen, no arms, no legs. Then suddenly it became less loathesome, as the sun glinted on the headlike portion, and it became apparent that the round blankness was merely a helmet. There was a sudden twitch of realization throughout the mob and perhaps a sigh of relief that this thing was not—not at first sight—a true monster; and first with a few stray excited chirrups, then full-throated male roars and excited female squeals, the crowd rocketed into the vocal equivalent of hysteria.

Down the metal ramp it glided, with a delicate ambulant motion, and it stopped by Jordan, who by now had lost whatever embarrassment he had showed, and when the striving police rammed through the crowd, clearing a lane to where Ngambi stood flanked by other officials at the building entrance, Jordan and the Gray One moved forward until they confronted each other, Earthman and alien. The crowd behind, with a delirious burst of energy, cracked the city police lines, and the uniformed UN security squadron barely held the last few feet until Ngambi's group made it through the doors of the building, with Jordan and the stranger at their heels.

The TV screen instantly blared forth with a commercial. My glass was empty and the bartender, not taking his eyes away from the TV for fear he would miss anything, gave me a refill and I realized that my breath was short and I felt sticky where I had been sweating.

It took several minutes for the welcoming committee to reach the main council room, and it was very satisfying to hear the idiotic comments and guesses made by the various "commentators," as they call themselves, and to know that any one of their guesses was no more valid than any of mine. The bartender, not wanting to miss anything, took the bottle off the backbar, and slid it between us. Let someone come in and try to get a drink while we were watching.

Then the screen changed again, and we were inside the council room. Every seat was taken, of course, with standees in the aisle too many for the security guards to evict all at once. In the left center stood Secretary Ngambi, Ken Jordan at the right, and in the center the gray alien, all roughly the same height. Under the concentrated TV light it could now be plainly seen that the grayness was a poncholike affair, no sleeves or slits or ornaments, and the globehead was truly some type of helmet, and I wondered absently how, if no one could see in, anyone could see out. Or did anything need to see out?

It was surprising how little whisper and bustle there was; an almost scared hush, quite unlike the exuberant shouting of the crowds outside who had known what they were cheering about. All this could not have taken more than a few breaths, and Ngambi raised his arms for attention—which he already had—and said, "Gentlemen ..." And suddenly it dawned on him he had absolutely nothing to say. Blankly he looked around for advice, for help, and then he regained some presence of mind. "Gentlemen," he said, waiving the elaborate phrases of office, "I think I will introduce Mr. Kenneth Jordan, of the United States. Mr. Jordan is, at present, our contact with our ... our foreign guest," and abruptly he sat down. Jordan, from looking interestedly around the council room, came to attention when he realized he was the center of eyes.

"Gentlemen," he said, clearing his throat sheepishly, "ladies and gentlemen," as he saw many women in his audience. "Er. Well! I'm Ken Jordan. I live in Detroit. That's in Michigan," belatedly. The alien moved, or rather its robe (uniform? armor? shimmered, and Jordan turned his head. There were sounds, almost inaudible, and Jordan turned again to face the audience and said, "Gentlemen—ladies and gentlemen—I'm supposed to introduce Captain Lee Kay Lukkari, captain of the cruiser KAYTA. Captain Lukkari is very impressed with the reception from the people of Earth for the first messenger . . . no, ambassador ... no ... I just don't know the word. Anyway, Captain Lee is the agent—or the representative of the Regan Club. I guess you'd better call it a group ... yeah, the Regan Group."

There was a short pause while he mused on this,

and then he turned to the alien. Soundlessly the top half of it swiveled back and forth, looking around the jammed council room, and seeming to calculate. Then suddenly bumps sprouted from its midsection upward, gripped the round headlike top, and I found myself holding my glass so hard it hurt, and the barman's breath beside me was wheezing with stress. There was motion, grayness swirling and sinking, and then the round helmet was gone and the gray masking was tossed aside. And I knew everything was a fake.

## Chapter Four

Captain Lee was human. Too solidly human, and the most unbelievably natural wonderful female ever seen outside of a fairy tale. So uniquely perfect that I knew at once that she was the end result of professional design. For a woman she was tall, probably five six or seven, weighing just enough in the right places, and her hair was the standard sleek platinum made boring by repeated presentation as a feminine sex symbol. Even the clothes were patently stagecraft: a silver blouse, silver breast ornaments—medals?—a wide silvery belt, and—so help me—silver-white kilts, only kilts aren't shorter than knee length. I expected to see a chorus of midgets skip in from stage right singing, "On the Good Ship Kaytapop," but it didn't seem to hit anyone else that way.

My bartender said, as she stood there for inspection, "Holy God," as a prayer; "just look at that!" He added something else which was drowned by the spontaneous bellow that slammed out of the overhead speaker when the UN audience got its breathing under control. Everyone in the council room was on his feet, including the women delegates and, oddly enough, the darker-skinned delegates, who might have been expected to resent that the first alien from outer space (which now I knew was a put-up job) turned out to be lily-white. Oh, I was impressed, all right; she was sexy enough to stir a lead lobster. But to have this Snow White lollypop emerge at this crucial moment was just too much like a stage setting sired by Lohengrin out of Hans Christian Andersen.

The shouting and whistles kept on—she indicated puzzlement, I think, when she heard the whistles, and Jordan leaned close and said something to her that made her smile—and I poured myself a drink out of the house bottle on the bar. The bartender didn't even know I took it. A thought struck me.

This show was due for a crash landing when Jordan "translated" for her. Just let him try "translating" nonsense syllables if she produced them; just let her try producing some exotic real language that she might know, and rest assured that someone, somewhere, would be able to understand it. But when the whooping and howling was finally shushed by Secretary Ngambi, she stood right up there to the mike and produced perfectly normal, perfectly natural phrases in a perfectly human voice, and her voice sounded as good as she looked and no one ever understood one solitary syllable. She turned and spoke softly to Jordan, who was basking in her glittery presence, and he cleared his throat importantly. Now he was the cheese that stood alone.

"She wants me to say this just like she's saying it," he prefaced. She stood easily, unselfconscious, a shapely sylph who knew her place was in the spotlight.

"I am Lee Kay Lukkari, captain of the cruiser KAYTA, envoy of the Regan Group. As the first representative of our group to touch down on your soil, I wish to extend you the best wishes of myself both as a person and as cruiser KAYTA's captain, and as the messenger of good will of the Regan Group.

"I may ease some curiosity by saying that this contact between two groups is the end result of a firm decision by our group to establish a communication with your groups."

There was a sharp intake of breath that we could hear even in the bar speaker.

"This visit, I can assure you, to me is a great personal honor. The hoped-for result of a lifetime of training. I have been specially trained for this visit, and it is my greatest . . . hope, desire, want that it will be of great value."

She was speaking in terse liquid-clear sentences, and slowly enough for Jordan to follow. I knew that someone would eventually identify the language she was using, and I wondered what it was. I had never heard anything quite like it, but on the other hand once I caught shortwave Japanese and thought it was Syrian.

Jordan kept doggedly one sentence behind her as she went on. "I regret that I cannot speak directly to you in a local language, but at present the technical difficulties are too great to overcome. I must hope you will accept the raw colors of my words and with your inside eye see the different hues I cannot now give you face to face."

Jordan was beginning to show strain. (It is not easy to translate rapid-fire fashion, they tell me. The UN interpreters earn every cent of their excellent salaries, and there aren't too many good ones around.) My bartender drank from his long-empty glass for the fifth time, looked vacantly surprised, and took his eyes away from the screen only long enough to see that I was pouring him a drink out of his own jug.

"After the time I, as cruiser captain, have observed

your world, there are many things I would like to know. Being of similar appearance and similar intelligence, I can assume you are equally curious. I suggest that for a limited time I try to answer whatever questions might be of most interest to you." As Jordan finished, she relaxed slightly and stood waiting.

As the import of the statement sank in, there was an instant hubbub, and Secretary Ngambi had to shut it up. First he bowed formally to the captain, spoke sharply to the effect that the captain had mentioned a limited time, and added that he would himself ask the first most obvious questions, and then permit others to do so, so that the captain would appreciate Earth courtesy.

"Captain Lee," he said, and she flashed him an impersonal beautiful smile as Jordan translated. Jordan's voice made her own language sound ugly. "Captain Lee, as secretary of this assembly it is my great pleasure. . . ." And he came up with rows of polite phrases. Then he got to the bone.

"Captain Lee, just where is your Regan Group? And this Regan Group: is it your home, your planet, perhaps?"

Her eyes were on the secretary as she hunted for words. "The Regan Group is a group, a club, a union, an association. It is composed of lots of very many planets in many different places. I do not know your methods of naming directions or your methods of measurement except very, very generally through Mr. Jordan, who is not trained in finding things. On a map of the various objects in your sky I am allowed to show you the approximate location of our Regan Group."

Ngambi jerked his head meaningfully, and an aide ducked to a desk microphone. Ngambi went on. "I will provide a star map. Perhaps you will tell us,

Captain Lee, why this particular time has been chosen—you did say that you have observed Earth for some time?"

This time she eyed Jordan while he was translating. He looked old and tired, working under unfamiliar mental strain, and I felt sympathy for the old drunk and what he had stood up to so far.

She said firmly, "This does not matter. The decision is not mine, but that of the Regan Group. I could not know all of the reasoning behind my mission to you, and my own feelings do not matter; I am here only to establish contact, to establish a minimum amount of communication; the decision is yours. Yours, all of your group's, their decision. Or, if you say the word, I will leave at once. For God's sake, can I get a drink?"

The last wail was, of course, Jordan's, who was by now a haggard jello. The captain looked at him questioningly when she heard the abrupt change in his voice, and he said something in her own language at which she smiled slightly. Ngambi's aid handed up a pitcher-glass-tray and Jordan needed only one look.

"Water?" he almost shouted. "I said a drink! Whaddya have to do to get a—" and he subsided as the captain touched his shoulder. He listened and said hopefully, "I suggest that there should be a short recess for a shot—for refreshments, and this discussion can be resumed for a limited amount of time."

Ngambi agreed at once, and as the TV crashed into the commercial the last thing we saw was the sheaf of reporters breaking loose from the press row and heading for the captain.

The broadcasts continued all that afternoon, some of the night, and all the next day while normal life slowed almost to zero. What happened was basically this:

Captain Lee demanded a decision on whether the

UN wanted to establish contact, and required her decision the next morning; only this much time, she indicated, was acceptable. It was a frustration-hell for the reporters and everyone else who wanted to talk or question because the only interpreter was Jordan, who demanded shots and beers until he hungered for cheeseburgers, which seemed to sober him back to coherency.

The captain's idea of communication was one-sided. She flatly stated that her mission was to collect a cross-section of Earth artifacts—not Jordan's words; he said "gadgets and art and stuff." There were other items that the Regan Group could purchase, since they would be strange, exotic, and pleasurable to Regans. The captain was blonde, beautiful, and blunt.

Purchase what? Ears pricked up at the UN.

Many items, unstated.

Purchase? With what?

The Regan Group would provide suitable means of exchange.

Purchase? How much?

As much as Earth would like to sell. And the roadblock came up.

This went on until she cut the barrage of questions, possibly out of pity for Jordan who was in rugged shape with his whiskey being rationed, certainly at Ngambi's orders. (All this time, someone noted, she never left the council room, inquired for the women's john, or showed any discomfort, providing much biological conjecture. Would Ngambi, as Earth spokesman, supply Jordan with anything he wanted? The captain said, through Jordan's fuzzy voice, that Mr. Jordan had suffered some discomfort and that, regardless of the UN's decision, Mr. Jordan would be repaid. Ngambi said, "Of course. . . ."

Ngambi escorted the captain back to the cruiser KAYTA, which somehow now looked too tinny to leap to the stars and which had rested silently in the same spot since high noon. The city police had barricaded it well, as they had been forced to do with all the gawkers shuttling around the edges of the UN Plaza, and she left Jordan and Ngambi at the metal ramp, accepting from Jordan the gray covering and helmet which he had refused to put down since she had removed them. The ramp flipped back to become part of the hull, and the cylinder went away, as simply as that. Straight up, not fast, not slow, no noise or commotion. Just straight up.

Someone had a directional mike, and we could hear Secretary Ngambi say, "All the way from the stars, Mr. Jordan, and such a tiny thing. . . ."

Jordan was almost drunk. He shook his head. "Hell, no; not in that. When I was in the Navy we'd call that the admiral's barge. I don't know where the cruiser KAYTA is."

# Chapter Five

The rest of the first act went on while I was two hundred miles north in Greenbush, where Mac had sent me back to work the next morning on the sensible grounds that a spaceship was one job and that espionage at Wurtsmith Airbase was another. Back behind the bar I went, trying not to be curt with the sympathetic customers who had heard of the sickness-in-the-family that had pulled me away for a couple of days, and I'm sure they forgave me the dopyness I showed at intervals; I couldn't help thinking about the KAYTA landing and what it really meant to us all. To my surprise, even though the TV and radio carried hardly anything but rehashes and conjectures re what had happened or what might, not one of my regulars or transients was worried enough to more than casually mention it. More than one flatly dismissed all the action of the last few days as a super advertising gimmick, even when the 6:00 P.M. doom-shouters became extra solemn and extra basso. All I could do was wash glasses, slice onions, make cheeseburgers, and agree with everybody.

This even on the next day, when the "admiral's barge" landed in the same place, disgorging the luscious Captain Lukkari to meet the same slobby Ken Jordan (who at least had had his work shirt and pants washed) and the same Secretary Ngambi. My pool players left their game long enough to make remarks about certain potentialities of the blonde Captain Kay, watched events for a placid few minutes, and finally drifted back to eight-ball. The back end of the bar, of course, demanded silence, that the TV be turned up louder and that the pool players shut up, but that was because they were tired of playing pinochle. I know the pouring rhythm for my regular's thirsts so I didn't miss much of the broadcast.

It was so short, so definite, and so neatly packaged that no one even thought to try picking up the soap.

The captain, through Ken Jordan, inquired if the UN wanted and would accept a representative. Secretary Ngambi, in several paragraphs, said yes. When he had finished, the UN floor showed enough enthusiasm to provide positive aural backing for the secretary. The blonde captain—damn, she *was* a dry-cell dream!—nodded calmly, and then whomped everybody flat on their butts by announcing, therefore, that the representative of the Regan Group would be Ken Jordan. Jordan was getting so dumbly used to translating that the fact was out before he recognized his own name. But the captain went on. This, of course, would be so only if Jordan would consent, and this, she admitted, would be a great responsibility, very great.

Jordan asked her something.

She explained, through Jordan, that it was the custom of the Regan Group to continue to work with their first contact. If Jordan chose to refuse, as he could and might, the Regan Group would then provide another representative. But this would take some time and effort, and the representative would not be an Earth person.

Secretary Ngambi asked the obvious question.

The captain said *she* had other jobs to do, and that left it up to Jordan.

Jordan looked at the captain, who smiled politely. Jordan looked at Ngambi, who looked vaguely guilty. Jordan looked around the packed council room, instantly got stage fright, and almost ran. But we're clever, we Yankees, we are.

The United States Ambassador popped up and got the floor because no one else had thought to ask for it. He congratulated Ken Jordan for having the sterling qualities native to all citizens of these great United States, asked him in the name of the United States to take the job offered him, and managed with two short sentences (before Secretary Ngambi and unanimous howls from the UN shut him up) to get over the idea that the Stars and Stripes should wave forever.

Jordan almost bashfully translated for her over the prompt Donnybrook (an important Russian was apparently being held down by his staff from trying to get at the completely justified collective smirks of the United States delegation). Captain Lee Kay Lukkari listened, glanced with no enthusiasm at the fracas out front, and lifted her eyebrows appealingly at Jordan. At the time, certainly, he had nothing else in mind but that unexpected appeal to patriotism he had just been sniped with. He nodded: I'm your man, Captain. And at this, that gorgeous doll reached over and patted this drunk on the head and her performing seal wiggled all over.

She spoke again, and even the Russian arguing vociferously with his fellows began to quiet down as Jordan tried to keep up with her. She thanked the

UN, she thanked Ken Jordan for accepting this unexpected load, she was certain that no one would regret any decision made today, but there were still minor clarifications to make. The Russian in the front row snarled angry Slavic at his harried restrainers, sat up sourly, and jerked his tie back around in front; the United States team relaxed—their man was in.

Mr. Jordan and the captain would return in—Jordan had to ask her details, counting on his fingers—twelve or thirteen days. This would be necessary, barely time enough to introduce Mr. Jordan to the details of his new job, and to the ... Jordan went back to her, and after some discussion came up with the phrase "and to the background structure and civilization of the Regan Group."

Furthermore, when they returned, Ken Jordan would be boss (Jordan brightened at the workman's word), and all contact with the Regan Group would be through him. His word would be final. Was this understood by all present?

In that case, said the captain, there was much to do and much to learn, and the UN would not consider her abrupt if she and Mr. Jordan left the meeting. ... The UN, at waves and gestures from Secretary Ngambi, stood politely and produced hearty cheers—except the Russians, who were all now unanimously agonized, having failed to get even a protest.

Jordan stood aside to let the captain lead the way, but she held back, and he turned to speak for her once more. "One more thing," he said. "As our representative, Mr. Jordan will give up his Earth citizenship and become a member of our Regan Group. We shall recite the formal rites when we return at the stated time." With Ngambi, they left at once.

Someone good was on the TV monitor that day. A split screen showed the dawning horror on the face of the United States section parallel with the idiotic glee that grew on the face of the head Russian. The background noise was so strong I couldn't hear it when the howling Russian used *both* his shoes to hammer his lectern, but I could see the faces of our standard allies like Canada and Great Britain. They thought it was equally hilarious. Smart Yankees, hey? Oh, hah, hah, hah.

When an Australian, with a big digger grin, took off one shoe to solemnly inspect his laces for the camera, I poured a shot and a bottle of Geyer's for the house before I turned off the TV.

Being two hundred miles away from a big city can have very definite advantages. There is no feeling of immediacy when newspapers are already a day late, the lag in printing even weekly magazines makes last week's happenings read like last year's, and like most everyone else I check in and out on the six o'clock TV news only long enough for the immediate catastrophes before the round of commercials. One of my retired regulars, however, used to trade me his weekly subscription to the Manchester *Guardian* and his daily mailed copy of the *Christian Science Monitor* (now, why would a retired chiropractor subscribe to the *Monitor*?) for an occasional double Irish and soda.

The *Monitor* mulled things over and presented several possibilities as ponderously as it usually does, and the *Guardian* did a much better job along the same lines, with the exception of restrained British glee with the American flag-waving cut down to half mast. Little one-inch items the *Guardian* reprinted from other national newspapers repeated the theme in twelve keys.

The *Alcona County Weekly* mentioned my trip to see ailing relatives and plugged the Potluck Dinner at the church hall; the Detroit newspapers rehashed their syndicated columnists into paraphrased editorials. *Time* used Captain Lee Kay Lukkari as Woman-of-the-Week superimposed on an idealized sketch of Ken Jordan; and *Life*'s spreads were impressive, beautiful, and pitifully querulous. All American media seemed proud that Jordan, as a United States citizen, had been selected as representative of the Regan Group and more than slightly miffed that Jordan was going to give up his citizenship. After the first few days, what had first been mentioned on the financial pages began to slide into the front sections; what did the Regan Group want, and how much? Looking back on the whole thing, it was like a small town waiting for tourist season to open. What's in it for me?

When the thirteenth day arrived, the world had been waiting since the twelfth. Cameras, lights, action, when they landed. Ngambi, Jordan, and the Captain Kay in the UN Chambers.

She looked different, but I don't know why. Jordan was off-tint, too, before I realized he was wearing the same work clothes, but now his clothes were silver-white, like the captain's. They had tailors on board the spaceship, because the pants fitted better.

Through Jordan, she again greeted and thanked the assembly. Then she and Jordan faced each other and spoke in short sentences which Jordan repeated after her, very slowly and very plainly.

"My name is Kenneth Jordan.

"I am a citizen of this planet.

"As of this instant, I give up all rights and duties as a citizen of this planet.

"As of this instant, I accept the duties and rights of a member of the Regan Group," and she turned partly to Ngambi and partly to the assembly as Jordan translated for her.

"This is enough ceremony for the Regan Group. Is it enough for your Earth Groups?"

Ngambi was helped by a burst of applause from the assembly that expanded until both Jordan and the captain were smiling. It lasted for many minutes while members of the various delegations crowded up and around to try to shake hands, to touch the captain and her new associates. Ngambi's shushing gestures helped calm them and the UN security police finally cleared the floor.

Then the captain herself spoke, with the grinning Jordan at her side. Her first words hit the assembly like a champagne firecracker:

"Thank you, members of Earth Groups."

And she wasn't speaking English, either. It was American, flat Midwestern, solid and nasal yet with a tricky background of accent.

"Thanks to Ken Jordan, now my associate, I have some knowledge of your way of speaking. I cannot say the words exactly how he says them as I have not enough time for practice—" And a voice from the gallery bawled, "Baby, you sound as good as you look!"

As the house exploded, you could see her digest the words and mentally translate them into her own speech. She laughed delightedly, and finally the noise died down and she went on.

"I am pleased you like me," and from anyone else it would have sounded affected. "But I must say this, that from the instant that Ken Jordan accepted his membership in our Regan Group I no longer have any authority or capability except as captain of the cruiser KAYTA. From now on I am his guest."

She stopped to think. The words were there, but

putting them together was a problem. I still knew something was wrong, because no one learns languages overnight even at Berlitz.

"As captain of the cruiser KAYTA, I have other duties I must perform elsewhere, and I am almost at the high tolerance of my schedule. But I can delay movement certainly until the sun—until this evening. Until then I wish to put aside my position as cruiser captain and be Lee Lukkari, to meet you as person to person, not person to group. I would like to talk to you, to listen to you, to say face to face how I am pleased to establish communications." She hesitated, flicked a glance at Jordan, who looked blank.

"We of the Regan Group do not use much formal ceremony. Ken Jordan is not knowing—not familiar even with your own ceremonies. Therefore I can suggest not as cruiser captain but as Lee Lukkari that I might experience what I have tasted in Ken Jordan's mind but not in reality—a shot and a beer."

When the TV cameras turned to other things I was still snickering, with my bar regulars. "A shot and a beer!" If that marvelous blonde started belting down boilermakers as Jordan had been doing all his life, that spaceship was going to drive itself home. (It turned out later, and I don't know who kept score, that she put away fourteen boilermakers, plus other national drinks like slivovitz, aquavit, and raki that were pressed on her by proud internationalists, and, possibly because of the appetizers that are always around at upper-crust soirees, managed to get no more than charmingly slugged.) It was with obvious regret that Ngambi ushered her to the spaceship, and, probably because TV had carried as much as they could of her during the afternoon, the crowds in the Plaza were her friends—every sweaty, yelling, whistling, prurient male, anyway. The spaceship went up and away, and I didn't notice at the time that Jordan hadn't bothered to see her off, nor apparently did anyone else—Jordan was already working on his job as representative of the Regan Group.

Somewhere around there must be a copy of the special 256-page issue that *Life* put out that next week, devoted solely to Ken Jordan, Captain Lee Kay Lukkari, and welcome-to-the-Regan-Group ads from General Motors, Mitsubishi, Siemens-Halske, and Weintraub Discount Distributors. It's full of color shots of Jordan and Ngambi, the Lukkari legs, the captain posing with Jordan. . . . The best shots were unposed, like the captain on a couch with her cheerleader legs tucked under her and her shoes alongside (a cross between Roman sandals and wedgies), Lukkari smiling and laughing, every single picture looking as though it came straight out of a posed cosmetic ad. She was so damned lovely it would make anyone mad, and to emphasize how attractive she was, how completely magnetic her looks, it was a grayhaired UN delegate from Austria who bowed over her hand and was the first to discover she had no little finger but another smaller thumb. It didn't shake him a bit; he didn't mention it right away, and when he did no one believed him, and only the pictures of her holding a glass proved he was right.

All that last afternoon she was listening, talking ever plainer with that tinkly indefinable accent, and *Life* published pages of data in question-and-answer form. Here are some of them.

Q: Captain Lukkari, how long did it take to teach Mr. Jordan your own language, and how long did it take to learn his?

A: I am not "Captain" while I am here. I am Lee Lukkari. "Mister" is an Earth title and I think Ken

Jordan will not want it anymore. To teach him our language, I cannot as yet translate numbers very fast without writing. But it would be a very small part of the time in which you would breathe once.

Q: And to learn his language?

A: The same, if I wanted to learn only that, but a little longer because I had to learn much more, as he did.

Q: You mean you both learned a new language in a fraction of a second—that is, less than a breath? How, may I ask?

A: I think the word is electric, partly.

Q: How is that done?

A: I will not say.

Q: Here is a star map, Captain Lukkari. Would you show us the location of your Regan Group?

A: Not Captain, Lee Lukkari. The Regan Group is in this area.

Q: We call that Alpha Centauri, Lee Lukkari. By our system of measurement the Regan Group is so far away it takes light almost five years to get there.

A: Yes.

Q: How long did it take you to get from your Regan Group to here?

A: I will not tell.

Q: Could you teach anyone here your language as fast as you did Mr. Jordan?

A: Yes.

Q: Lee Lukkari, I am an etymologist, a specialist in languages. Would you teach me your Regan Group language?

A: No. There is no need. Ken Jordan is Regan Group representative.

Q: Would he teach me if I asked him?

A: He does not have my cruiser equipment. You would have to learn it like a baby, by speaking, and I do not think he would even if he could, as he is not patient. Why do you wear hair on your face while you are still young?

Q: Why did you choose Ken Jordan as your Regan Group representative?

A: It is customary. If our first contact had declined, I would have passed on my command as cruiser captain and studied until I myself would be able to be our representative. This would take much time.

Q: But you said you have equipment to teach and learn very fast, in less time than a breath.

A: You do not understand. It is permissible first for the Regan Group to impress our language upon another, but to trade minds is a decision that must be made by the other person.

Q: Did you say to trade *minds?*

A: Yes. It is a heavy decision to become another person.

Q: Do you mean you are now Ken Jordan, and he is you?

A: Not in our bodies, of course. But I know and have experienced everything he has done or thought of in the past, and he is now, as much as me, cruiser captain.

Q: But Ken Jordan is a man!

A: Our first contacts usually are male. The male is the explorer, the searcher, the defender, the leader, except in rare cases which I have read in books.

Q: But you are a woman.

A: Yes. Our Regan Group has found that the female is best equipped to supply knowledge, to let herself be drawn on for background, to . . . to submerge her personality for the new first contact. This is not easy, and although I have been trained specifically for the first contact, and although I have had thirteen days to absorb Ken Jordan, I still have water boiling in my brain, if I say that right.

Q: How does Ken Jordan feel? How did he feel about . . . about changing brains with you?

A: I think he feels ashamed, a little, as I do. Would you like anyone else to know everything you have ever thought or done? I feel this way, even though I have been trained to disregard this, because I am a person—and I am a woman. Is any liquid that is served in a container like this called a "shot"? Ken Jordan did not know.

Q: I came back, Lee Lukkari, to tell you I grew this beard to help me in my work. Can I ask you your words for mother, father, son, daughter?

A: You are a specialist in words, you said, and I think I know why you ask, because these are the same words in most languages. I will not now say, but if you will later tell Ken Jordan that Lee Lukkari thinks it would be fair, he will tell you much more than you can think to ask now.

Q: Why does your Regan Group need a representative on Earth?

A: We do not "need" anything in that sense. Ken Jordan once read a book about climbing a mountain because it was there; it made such little sense to him that he remembered it and so I now remember it. I hope you understand.

Q: Why are you laughing?

A: Ken Jordan said he walked into my auxiliary "because it was there," and could not compare it to a mountain to be climbed.

Q: Your "auxiliary"; this is your ship you landed in?

A: Yes. Ken Jordan had that word in his head.

Q: Where is your cruiser KAYTA?

A: I will not tell.

Q: Can you tell us something about the navy of the Regan Group?

A: I know Ken Jordan was in your Earth navy; he disliked it more than any member of the Regan Group, but for different reasons. Our Regan Group has no navy as you know it.

Q. But you are captain of the cruiser KAYTA. No navy?

A: I must study the books Ken Jordan will supply before I can give a true answer. My cruiser travels, searches, explores. It reports, solves, measures. . . . I cannot explain.

Q: You are very beautiful, Captain Lukkari.

A: Not captain, Lee Lukkari. Thank you. Much of my selection for the first contact was because of my appearance.

Q: Would you explain that a little more fully?

A: I will not explain.

Q: Your clothes; are they worn by members of the Regan Group?

A: Of course not. I am a cruiser captain. In my cruiser I wear much different clothes, depending upon where I am and what I am doing.

The questions and answers, as reported by *Life*, went on and on. Secretary Ngambi ran interference while escorting her around the UN building, in which she seemed singularly uninterested. She was equally polite to the delegates from Tanzania, Portugal, and Finland, to the questioners from Tass, Reuter's, and the United Press; she did not care for martinis, but was enthusiastic about anchovy olives; she was fingering-curious about the materials used in Jordanian djellabas and Indian saris; she made a face at caviar and Turkish Delight, but enjoyed Lebanese crackers and French Roquefort; she scribbled countless autographs with an emphatic mark that looked like a sinebar; she expressed pleasure at the different drinks that were offered her, all of which she drank slowly and carefully; and as the liquid intake increased she used the female retiring room with normal frequency. *Life* reported, presumably accurately, that under her uniform skirt, fastened to the front of her right thigh, was a tiny case for feminine essentials. Completely efficient essentials, as when she left the UN at close to sundown she still looked as though she was fresh from a beauty shop. Later issues of *Vogue* and *Teen Topics* dwelt upon this at some length.

Then she was gone.

She hadn't received all the attention. Ken Jordan had crowds around him, too. He had been equally surly to the press and to the United States and Russian delegates, had switched from shots and beers to plain beer, and had finally shouldered his way to Secretary Ngambi to whom he put several direct questions. He and Ngambi had gone into Ngambi's private apartment and a few minutes later a third man had entered, with Ngambi leaving almost at once to return to playing host to Lee Lukkari.

When the third man left, some time later, he was identified as head of the delegation from Switzerland; Ken Jordan, even in his quickly recognizable white shirt and pants, somehow got out of the UN building and was next identified by a *Times* legman at Kennedy Airport as Jordan was boarding a Swissair jet. Disbelieving his eyes, the *Times* legman strolled to the Swissair counter and suddenly realized from the indignant passenger conversation that a whole flight had been canceled with no advance notice and that, if Jordan was bound for Switzerland, the *Times* had better get in on it. He called his city desk.

A *Times* stringer was waiting when the Swissair jet landed near Geneva, but the jet was tractored direct into Maintenance and the *Times* man—although a native Swiss—was ushered back to his home by ultra-polite Swiss police when he tried to follow. Back in New York, Ngambi shrugged and said that Ken Jordan was probably vacationing after the high-pressure events of the past few weeks, and did anyone think that he wasn't entitled to a rest?

Remembering that with Captain Lukkari now out of reach and the world's newspapers and magazines featuring Jordan as the sole emissary of an alien civilization, it is surprising that it took eight days for Jordan to be spotted—white shirt and pants and all—by a retired East Lansing schoolteacher in a *bierstube* in something-dum-Kirchen. Jordan at once admitted his identity, said he was going back to Detroit the next day, signed autographs and posed for snapshots all around, bought drinks for the house, and left, beered to the ears, with two escorts who had been keeping in the background until he rose to go.

The next afternoon, an unscheduled Swissair jet landed Jordan at Detroit and a cab took him to the Statler, where he holed up on the entire sixteenth floor with uniformed Burns guards at both stairways and the elevators, plus a well-stocked portable bar. And this is where Mac, my boss, tossed me right into the middle of the lions.

He—Mac—pulled me out of my Greenbush bar with no notice to my local boss. "Forget it," he said. "Damn the sergeant, damn the airbase. Get down here as soon as you can. Now, scramble!"

When I walked into the smelly Detroit agency Mac was waiting. I had rarely seen him so upset before.

"All right. Sit down and listen. You know this Ken Jordan is back in Detroit?"

I nodded. "It was on TV."

"Good," and he slid the ashtray to where I could reach it. "He's hitting the bottle heavy. He ordered a secretary yesterday from Kelly Girls and she was lucky to get out with her clothes on. Today, five hours from now, he's going to have a male Kelly Girl."

I grinned. Now I knew where Jimbo was.

"That's right," Mac said.

"Jimbo is the new male secretary that reports for work five hours from now, but Jimbo is not going to work out."

"No?" I said. "Why not?"

Mac grunted. "Not enough smoke on the ball. But you have."

"Look, Jimbo's a friend, Jimbo's been around a long time—"

"Look, hell," Mac snarled at me. "Listen one lousy

minute. Jimbo is not the man for the job. Right now Jordan is one step out of this world, and I can stay one step ahead of him all the way. How would it be if I had the only pipeline into this Regan Group—and you were the pipeline? No FBI, no CIA, no Counter-intelligence, just you!"

"Just me, reporting to you. And I know who *you* want to report to."

Mac leaned back in his chair. "The Man in Washington. Maybe report direct—maybe a whole new setup."

"With you in charge?"

A chuckle. "Who else?"

I stubbed out my cigarette. "You thought of this all by yourself."

He admitted it. "And we've got to make it fast. So far we're the dead end department everyone forgot, but I happen to know there's a crew flying in tomorrow—today—all brass, all from Washington, all empire-builders. Once I get you in, we're *in;* everything comes through you—and goes out through me."

"Who's an empire-builder now?"

"I am," and he sobered suddenly, to stare me in the eye. "I'm a GS-12. I've been passed over twice for upgrade."

I hadn't known that.

"I'm stalled," he said flatly. "I can't quit because of my pension, and after twenty-two years they can't fire me. But they can make me so miserable I wish I was dead. For eight years they can put me in Coconino County or a four-by-six office in Rock Island," and I knew that all this was quite possible.

"You're making Ken Jordan sound pretty important," I said after a moment.

Mac chewed a knuckle while he thought. "Hell," he said finally, "you might as well know it all. While

Jordan was in Switzerland the last few days, this—damned spaceship landed at one of the Swiss military airports and dumped off hundreds of cubes of stuff covered with some kind of plastic. One of the cubes fell off a lift truck and had to be lifted back with a crane—and the cube isn't even two feet across. What do you think is that heavy?"

"Lead?" I asked politely.

Mac showed his teeth. "Lead, maybe. But most of the cubes went into a Swiss Army cave and the rest went into the Swiss government vaults!"

"Gold? There isn't that much gold in the world."

Mac was triumphant. "Exactly—not that much gold in the world. But if those cubes are all gold it's so many billions of dollars I don't believe it myself."

I didn't bother to ask Mac where the facts came from. He's been around the federal system a long time.

He didn't quite plead with me. He's too bullheaded for that. "I know," he said. "This could be a pipedream. But if that bum has got that much money to spend he could play all kinds of merry hell just leaving it on deposit to draw interest, even with the Swiss neutral. If I can get you in with Jordan, if you can stay in with him, just to keep me—us—informed . . . Can't you just see the Reds or the limeys begging *us* for *our* data?"

And they would, come to think of it. All right, put the cards on the table. "What's in it for me?"

He knew he had me. "You know what I'm shooting for," and it was not a question.

Sure, I knew. "The highest slot on any list."

"Right! As high as I go you'll go right with me, one step behind. One step behind—if we make it in with Jordan."

"Mac," I said honestly, "why me?"

He had to tell the truth. "Because you're all I have available. Jimbo couldn't swing it. He might get in, but he couldn't stay. You, you're smart. You know you won't get much higher; you were lucky even to work up to GS-9. You've got the looks, the personality, the brains to think ahead," and he began to laugh quietly. "You can tell bigger lies than anyone else I ever knew with a straight face because I OK your expense accounts. Now how about it?"

I hung over the edge. "What happens if I don't get in? What happens if I get in and can't swing it? What happens if someone else has made plans and I mess it up? You did say a crew was on the way from Washington."

"Yes. I don't know why, but they'll have their own ideas. If you blow the lid, you were acting on my direct orders. I take the rap. I used my judgment. I was the man on the spot and I made a bad guess. Nothing happens to you. I take the rap. After twenty-two years they can't fire me."

No, but they could make him wish they would.

"How about it?" He stood up. "Yes or no?"

I shrugged. "Why not? You told me what to do and I did it. You take the rap."

He reached for his coat and flicked off his desk lamp. "Let's go somewhere else for a few hours," and again he was Mac the Boss. "If nobody can find us nobody can tell us what not to do. You, you're supposed to be two hundred miles away, and who cares?"

After he shooed out the lone derelict sleeping it off in the outer office I said, "Mac, you seem pretty sure I can get in to Jordan. The TV says the sixteenth floor has Burns guards at the elevators and both stairways."

Mac locked the outer door and smiled pleasantly.

"You knew we had a girl on the Statler switchboard." Well, the government did, but Mac would have alerted her to his special needs even though she had her own boss to report to.

"Coincidence." He was still pleased by his own luck. "The office manager at Kelly Girls is a guy I went to school with in Albany; he let me get Jimbo in tomorrow morning. As for getting into this Jordan, the Burns guard at the door is Jimbo's brother-in-law."

"My," I said admiringly, "you are lucky. Lucky and brave and—"

"Shut up," he said without heat. "I'd have found an angle. I would have had to," and we spent the next few hours in my own apartment checking out details.

At exactly nine-fifty that morning I took a Statler elevator to the eleventh floor, walked up four flights and rested for a few minutes, and then walked up one more. At the sixteenth-floor landing excited men and women were arguing with a stolid Burns guard, and at nine-fifty-nine one of the men slugged the Burns guard, who slid halfway across the landing. The small crowd instantly poured in the door, except for one man who threw himself on the groggy guard, and flowed down the hall to the door where another Burns patrolman was standing, and at the other end of the hall a third guard appeared from his station.

Jimbo's brother-in-law tensed himself, dived headlong at the small yelling group, tumbled them while handing off a neat lateral to my waiting hand. His job done, he flailed about with a will while I wondered just how many of the mob were Mac's stooges. As I managed to get the key into Jordan's door the third Burns guard came running down the hall to join the fight, with another smaller group tailing him. Then the key turned, I palmed it and slid inside the Jordan suite.

Attracted by the muffled thumps outside, both Jordan and Jimbo were standing, Jimbo at a typewriter and Jordan half erect from a lounge chair. Jordan was unshaven and ugly, Jimbo was wearing his panicky look. I said nothing, just stood there, panting excitement all over, back against the door, letting Jordan look things over.

"All right," Jordan said in an oddly mild tone, "just what the hell do you want, sexypants?"

## Chapter Six

I said, "I'm looking for a job, Mr. Jordan."

Jordan grunted. "Yeah? Doing what?"

"Anything," I said. "I can type, I can take shorthand, I can run an office, I can file."

He walked over to his portable bar, poured himself a drink, and went back to sit on the edge of a coffee table to glower at me. "How did you get past the guard at the door?"

"He got rushed and I sneaked past him while he was trying to get everybody out."

He stopped his drink halfway to his mouth. "Get everybody out?"

"They wouldn't let me off the elevator so I got off at a different floor and walked up. Somebody—there was a crowd at the door—got past the guard at the stairway and we all ran in. I ducked the guard at your door and here I am." Past Jordan I could see Jimbo winking at me while he practiced his worried look; outside the room door the thumps had quieted somewhat.

Jordan put down his glass, walked again to the portable bar and brought back a bottle, and this at ten o'clock in the morning. "How do you spell 'encyclopedia'?"

I spelled it for him.

He poured another drink. "You said you could type. Lemme see you type."

I went over to Jimbo, who shrank out of my way, and ran off a few lines on the typewriter as fast as I could: "I am in the suite of Mr. Kenneth Jordan, who, I hope, will give me a job; I can spell, I can type, I can take shorthand, and I am smart enough not to make the same mistake twice." Then I got up to hand him the sheet of paper.

He read it, went back for a reread, and then grinned at me. He looked better that way.

"You," he snarled at Jimbo, "you're fired. Go on back and tell your boss to send me a bill after they teach you to spell 'encyclopedia,'" and while Milquetoast Jimbo was sidling nervously toward the door, Jordan turned back to me. "Hell, if I could spell it I wouldn't need that jerk."

Jimbo opened the door to leave, a guard's face showed, and Jordan promptly snarled at him. "Shut the door, stupid!" There was a minor hassle while Jimbo struggled to get out against the guard's pulling the door shut. It was settled by Jordan, who shoved Jimbo away from the door, yanked it open with the outside guard still clinging to the doorknob, pushed poor Jimbo out, and slammed shut the door.

Muttering to himself, Jordan went back and perched again on the coffee table. "Write this down," he said. "Encyclopedia. A couple of dozen."

I was ready with a sheet of typing paper.

There was a long silence and I looked up. Jordan was frowning blackly at the wall. I clicked the typewriter space bar a few times and he swiveled his glance at me.

Abruptly he said, "How would you go about getting in to see the mayor of Windsor?"

"Windsor, Ontario? Mr. Jordan, you'd have no trouble. I think he'd be honored if you took him to lunch."

"He would?" This seemed to surprise him.

"Would you like me to arrange it?" I asked in my best professional voice.

"Sure," he said. "I sure would."

I reached for the desk telephone. "Mr. Jordan's suite," I told the hotel operator. "Can you connect me with the office of the mayor of Windsor, Ontario?" While the call went through I made businesslike preparations with pencil and paper. "I'm calling for Mr. Kenneth Jordan of the Embassy of the Regan Group. Mr. Jordan would like to discuss several important matters with His Honor the Mayor. Would it be possible for His Honor to have lunch with Mr. Jordan, say tomorrow?" I wiggled my eyebrows at Jordan, nodded eagerly. "Yes, I can hold. Thank you."

As Jordan started to speak I slid my hand over the mouthpiece. "How did you know I had important matters to discuss?" he asked suspiciously.

I gave him my honor-bright smile. "It figures. If you want to talk to any mayor it's going to be important."

He thought that over and then agreed. "It figures. Yeah, it figures."

The mayor's secretary came back on the line. "Of course, any time would be satisfactory," I said. "Say, tomorrow at one o'clock? Mr. Jordan will be at His Honor's office at one. One moment, please."

Jordan was making faces at me. "Nobody else, just the mayor, understand?"

I went back to the telephone. "Mr. Jordan," I went on smoothly, "would at least for the present prefer a personal chat with His Honor. Could this be done, on a man-to-man basis, with no publicity? Mr. Jordan will appreciate your courtesy, and will be glad to meet His Honor anywhere. You will call back? Thank you again."

I put down the telephone and turned to Jordan. "The mayor's secretary will call back in a few minutes with a definite meeting place that's very private."

Jordan was curious. "How did you know how to work this so quick?"

"Mr. Jordan, I doubt there's anyone in the world that can read or watch TV that doesn't know who you are. I think it's quite possible he may end up asking you for your autograph."

Jordan liked that. His sudden notoriety had apparently not yet sunk all the way in. Suddenly he said, "You're a pretty smart babe."

Well, maybe so. "After all, Mr. Jordan, I used to be office manager for a tire business, even if it was pretty small." The honest look again. "Even if I did get fired."

He laughed outright at that and was not impressed. "Wish I had a dollar for every time I got fired." He upended the bottle over his glass, found it empty, and went to the bar to open another. Almost absently he said, "What did they fire you for? Nobody ever fired a doll like you without a good reason."

I'd been hoping for that question. "I broke my boss's nose with a paperweight. He thought I was a different kind of a doll."

He choked briefly with his glass to his mouth. "With a paperweight!"

"I couldn't lift a typewriter."

He began to laugh and laugh and went over to a lounge chair to enjoy the paperweight, taking his bottle and glass with him. The more he thought about it the funnier it seemed to him, and I sat quietly and catalogued him.

Height, five ten or eleven. Weight, two hundred plus, mostly around the center. Complexion, fair to sallow. Age— I remembered the description given me in the Triangle Bar, and it was accurate—he could be anywhere from forty to sixty. Bluntly, he looked terrible.

He hadn't shaved that morning, to begin with. His skin was blotchy with fine red lines at the cheekbones that checked with alcohol and high blood pressure. When he held his glass there was a faintly visible tremor. His hair was graying at the edges, and this alone added years to his age. The white pants and shirt were absolutely filthy; the shoes—I repressed a double take as I realized the shoes were the Roman sandal type worn by his Captain Lukkari. And they were also filthy. He had a faint transverse scar across his chin, and the skin around his eyes pouched down like the skin of an alligator; his kidneys were probably also shot.

The telephone rang importantly. It was the mayor of Windsor's secretary, who suggested the St. Clair Inn, on Wyandotte, not the men's bar but the dining room. At one o'clock? Right, and thank you. I turned back to Jordan, who was still chuckling about my paperweight. I didn't think the story was really that funny.

"Mr. Jordan," I said. "Mr. Jordan."

He focused on me. "Yeah."

"Am I hired? Am I going to work for you?"

He considered it. "Why not?"

"Then I can talk to you as I used to talk to my boss?"

Agree he did. "But not with no paperweight! Bust my nose and I'll bust yours," and I think he would.

"Mr. Jordan, are you going to meet the Mayor of Windsor dressed like that?"

He was unworried. "Plain water'll wash everything. Don't even need soap."

I kept after him. "If you meet the mayor in those white pants and shirt you'll be recognized right away."

"So I wear a coat." Stubbornly: "These are my clothes and I wear Regan clothes from now on. So do you if you work for me. Regan clothes."

They'd be clean, if I did. "Don't you think the representative of the Regan Group can afford more than one shirt and one pair of pants?"

He was getting annoyed. "Hell, you sound like my ex-wife. So I'll buy more pants and shirts."

"You can call a tailor. He'll measure you right here, make whatever you want, and you won't have to leave this room."

Anything to shut me up. He agreed, I got on the telephone, and in minutes Hudson's was eager to send over their top men's fashion designer and a choice of materials. I didn't dare tell Jordan about the "fashion designer," and could only hope Hudson's wouldn't send a swish.

There were no trays or dishes around. Had Mr. Jordan had breakfast yet? No, he hadn't had breakfast yet and never ate breakfast, but he could use a cheeseburger after he finished his drink. Drink? The bottle was half gone, and his tongue was getting thicker by the minute. I called room service, ordered a small steak with every possible trimming, informed the Statler desk that Hudson employees would be showing up shortly, and agreed I would also alert the Burns guard outside the door. Jordan was by now half dozing in his lounge chair. I opened the door, announced to Jimbo's brother-in-law that any J. L. Hudson people with identification should be admitted, winked at him, and went back inside snickering at the beautiful black eye he would be wearing very shortly. Jordan was by now snoring lightly and for the next half hour I sat staring at this representative of an alien civilization.

When room service delivered the steak I managed to get him awake enough to eat first a few bites and then as he woke up he began to eat methodically until the tray was bone-clean. The Hudson duo showed up just as he finished: a little rotund man with a busy tape measure and a taller fussy man with a sheaf of material samples. Jordan had to be reminded that he was the one who had ordered clothes, and I listened with some amusement as he defined exactly what he wanted. White shirts, pants, nothing else, just like the ones he was wearing. He held reasonably still for the tape measure (the little fitter was at once interested in the Regan material of the clothes Jordan was wearing and managed to convey his curiosity to the taller man), waved away the book of samples proffered for his choice, ordered me to pick out the correct material (which I did: a heavy, white, very expensive flannel), and ended up by demanding an open sports-type collar. Then when the taller man admitted he had seen the blonde Captain Lukkari and the way she had been dressed, Jordan told him to make me the identical clothes. Knowing the skirt styles hadn't been short since the later sixties, I wondered if the scar on my left hip would show and what else was going to come up on this deal.

When all was finished Jordan weaved for the portable bar again and I excused myself long enough to usher out the fitters, grin back at the Burns guard's black eye, which was now growing beautiful, and get back inside after specifying that maybe Jordan was satisfied but if anyone was going to measure me for clothes it would be a woman. This disappointed the stubby fitter, but he promised to send me a lady tailor. I told him I'd be measured in private and I'd be over to the store later. When the guard let me back in with his own key (of which I had the mate), Jordan was sitting again in his lounge chair, again with his bottle.

"Stand over there," he said. "All right, now turn around. All right, sit down. No, I just got a coupla things to get straight." I sat up straight and looked primly interested.

"You been around."

Had I?

"Sure you have. I heard the way you talked on the phone. The way you talked to these clothes fellas. You said you used to be an office manager where you worked."

I asked him if he wanted references, names, places?

"Hell, everybody phonies up references. Every job shop in town's got a different set of mine. If they need a shaper hand I'm a shaper hand; if they need a slotter man, that's me; if they need a jig-borer, I spent ten years on a Pratt and Whitney. No grinders—all grinder hands are nuts. But I been thinking over what I gotta do. I can hunt around and find somebody, sure, but all I'd have to go on would be references, and they could be just as big lies as the application blanks I used to fill out. You really want a job?"

I looked him in the eye. "Yes, Mr. Jordan. I need the money. I'm used to working for a living," and all of it was true.

He hefted his bottle, put it down untasted. "OK. You got the job, but I already said that, didn't I? I gotta have somebody I can have do something without me telling them how. You know— Say, what's your name, anyway?"

"Dana Iverson. Mrs. Dana Iverson."

He looked up sharply. "You married? Your husband working?"

"No," I said. "No husband. Divorced."

He laughed without humor. "You been around the track, too. Well, Dana Iverson—now, what kind of a name is that?"

"My father read it in a book. I'm supposed to be a blonde Viking."

He raised his eyebrows. "And you're a redhead."

"This year I am, Mr. Jordan."

"Hey," thinking about it. "No more of this Mr. Jordan stuff. Just Ken Jordan. No names or stuff like that, because I haven't got any title. Just Ken Jordan. That's the way they—we do it in the Regan Group. What was I gonna say? Yeah. I gotta have somebody around me that if I want something I get it, or if I want to find out something I don't have to tell them how.

"That's because I can run any toolroom machine I ever saw, but that's all. I started college once, but they flunked me out; it wasn't a very good college or they wouldn't have let me in in the first place. But I gotta have somebody that if they don't know what I want they can find out. OK?"

"I understand, Mr.— I mean, Ken Jordan. I think I told you I don't make the same mistake twice."

Jordan got up, placed his bottle accurately on the bar, and went to stare out the window. You get a good view from the sixteenth floor of the Statler. He came back to pace around the room.

Then, "I got another reason, Dana Iverson. I always worked in a shop. Out where the work is, where the girls in the office only come out to get the big boss to answer his phone calls. The girls, they hold their dresses back, they say hello and they smile and they go back in the office and make faces when they wipe the oil and chips off their shoes. They punch their time clocks and they get in the boyfriend's car that probably isn't paid for and it has only a dollar's worth of gas in the tank but he works in a white shirt and he doesn't have cast iron chips ground into his skin. ..."

He planted one foot on the coffee table. "Well, I got a good job now. No more grease all over the tub when I take a bath, no changing clothes in the hall when I come home from work. And every babe that works for me is going to have class. You got it, babe, class. Otherwise you'd have been out the door faster than you came in. You got the looks, you got ... hell, you got brains, probably. You know a lot more about things than I do; I know toolshop and that's all. You see what I mean?"

I felt sorry for the poor beast. His voice, by the time he had finished, had been almost whining. I had a very good hunch, which later turned out to be true, that he had once married one of those "girls from the office." I didn't know what kind of answer he wanted me to give, so I sat quiet while he sat and felt sorry for himself.

Then he perked up. Businesslike: "You still wear Regan Group clothes. Everybody wears Regan clothes that works for me."

I couldn't resist it. "Like a uniform? Like Captain Lee Lukkari? I thought it wasn't a navy."

He looked up at my reference to the blonde captain and his face clouded over momentarily. "Lee Lukkari ..." Then to my astonishment he produced as evil a leer as I've seen. "Hell," he said happily, "she doesn't wear that kind of clothes all the time, just when she landed in New York. She just wore clothes like that because I told her that was what Earth Groups would like to see. Kid, she damn near froze to death until she rigged built-in heaters—she comes from a warm place."

Built-in heaters? Where, under that skirt and blouse, did she put them?

"Besides," and the idea convulsed him, "I like short skirts. The babes that work for me wear short skirts, the shorter the better, starting with you. "But," he warned me, "don't you ever let that out. Everybody in the Regan Group wears short skirts while I'm around."

He thought I was serious when I said I thought that, to be consistent, he should wear kilts.

"Nope," he said. "But in the summer time, shorts. With no collars and no ties all year round. No more sweat running down your legs, no itchy pants in the summer, no choke-collars when you get dressed up. . . ." He dwelt lovingly on how now he could wear what he wanted when he wanted, and people couldn't say a word because he was wearing Regan Group clothes. Like the hat the Turks wear.

"Want a drink?" He changed the subject.

"Thanks, Ken Jordan. Not while I'm working." And the telephone rang exactly on cue.

"Embassy of the Regan Group," I said. It was the Statler manager, who showed surprise when he heard my feminine voice.

"I know Mr. Jordan left positive orders that there were to be no visitors, especially the press—but to whom am I speaking, please?"

I smiled inwardly. "This is Ken Jordan's administrative assistant speaking. Not Mr. Jordan, Ken Jordan. This is Mrs. Iverson."

The manager coughed politely. "I see. Mrs. Iverson,

this is rather important, and I thought that despite Mr. Jordan's instructions—"

"Ken Jordan," very firmly.

"I'm so sorry. Despite Ken Jordan's instructions, I feel he should know that there is a rather highly placed gentleman in the Department of State—"

I was enjoying this. Ken Jordan could see it in my face, came over, and I tilted the earpiece so that he could hear both our voices as he crowded close. He needed a bath.

"The Department of State? Which Department of State?"

The manager's voice was outraged anguish. Probably someone was at his ear, like Jordan at mine. "Why, our own—the United States Department of State. He prefers not to give his name, but he would like to see Ken Jordan on a matter of pressing interest. He assures me—"

Jordan was waggling his head. I said, "Would you hold for one moment while I check with Ken Jordan?"

Jordan, shaking his head even more wildly, was surprised to see me put down the telephone and pose quietly. Then he began to understand and began to snort so loud I had to cover the telephone mouthpiece. In precisely two minutes I picked up the phone again.

"I'm sorry, sir, so very sorry. But Ken Jordan cannot possibly see anyone today. If the—the anonymous gentleman would leave his name and where he can be reached, perhaps tomorrow or the next day?" I could close my eyes and see the Statler manager in turn visualizing Ken Jordan so busy with the portable bar. "I'm very sorry, but now you must excuse me." I must admit everything was comic—imagine hanging up on the Department of State! It helped Jordan to laugh and I felt better. Maybe this job was going to be fun at that.

Jordan said, "Take off, Dana Iverson. No," when he saw the look on my face, "no troubles. Be here tomorrow about eight. I get up early. I got a lot of things for you to do, and now I just feel like relaxing and getting loaded. What are you looking at me like that for?"

"Do you really want me to say?"

"Why not?"

I said, "It's barely noon. Tomorrow you have a lunch appointment with the Mayor of Windsor, you need a good night's sleep tonight, and I'm certain a lot could be done if you really want to." I cut off the forming frown by adding, "And I just got this job. I want to keep it. And I'd like to know some of these things I'll have to get, or to know, to keep the job."

"Damn," he finally said, "you're working to getting bounced out on your ear. My ex-wife used to be right all the time, too. All right, babe, if you wanna work I can work too. A cold shower will put me ready to think," and spoiled the effect by glugging a healthy swig before he headed for his shower. I'm convinced that anyone who takes cold showers can be nothing but insane.

But a cold shower did sober him, and when I left that afternoon, with Jordan swilled and out cold in his lounge chair, to meet Mac, my real boss, and bring him up to date on events, I had a long, long list of things I had to get, to do, and to find out.

# Chapter Seven

This, if I remember right, was on a Wednesday. Thursday evening there was a meeting.

It was in a sales suite at the Harper-Connors Holiday Motel. Mac met me at the door when I knocked, ushered me politely to a straight-backed customer's chair, and when I saw where Mac's chair was in the line of seniority it wasn't hard to see that my boss was in the middle of his own bosses.

"This is Mrs. Iverson," Mac said. "Iverson, this is Mr. Waldron. You've met before."

You bet we had. Waldron, Mac's boss and mine, didn't believe in women in any grade above GS-4, and if he hadn't been on his month and a half annual leave when the vacancy opened I'd still be a GS-7. But I nodded pleasantly, just the same.

"Mr. Herman, Department of State."

Herman was swarthy, smiling, and from his chair's position not quite as close to God as he'd like to be.

"This is Mr. Sawyer, Department of Commerce."

Sawyer was big, ruddy, balding, and looked like a successful used-car dealer. So he had two strikes on him already.

"This is Mr. Bolio. You've met."

Yes, we had. The local resident agent of the FBI.

"And this," with the proper air of humility, "is Mr. Farber, Department of State."

Farber was about third down in the hagiology of Washington. A career man, not too well known publicly, he had lasted out four presidents and two political administrations. There were at least four other attendees in the background, but if they weren't important enough to be introduced I didn't care who they were.

Farber—and the instant I heard his voice I knew why he had never tried to run for office: it was high tenor, nasal, and much too Back Bay even for Wellesley—said, "You forgot your halo, Mrs. Iverson."

That startled me, which most things don't.

He smiled toothily. "I'm not exaggerating, Mrs. Iverson. You represent an angelic appearance to all of us. You seem to be the only way in God's earth right now that we might be able, first, to obtain a line of insight into Ken Jordan's murky medulla and, second, to possibly influence his thinking—if you'll excuse the word—and, third, if he cannot be influenced or swayed, to provide advance notice of what course this unbelievably lucky atavist intends to pursue. You do not agree with me, Mrs. Iverson?"

Farber had cuaght some expression on my face. I took my time answering. "I don't know whether I disagree with you or whether I don't, Mr. Farber. About the line of insight and about influencing him . . . Right now I just started a new job. I can tell you what he wants right away or in the next few days. The part about the murky medulla and the atavism—no. Ken Jordan is no dummy. He's shrewd, uneducated certainly, but shrewd. He knows what he has even if he doesn't know exactly what he's going to do with it. Yet maybe he does know."

Farber's eyes narrowed. "You have a reason for that last statement, Mrs. Iverson?"

"I don't know," I said honestly. "Here is a list of the things he wants right away. Carbon copies," and to keep Mac in the hierarchy handed Mac the carbons and let him pass one to Farber's outstretched hand.

Farber flicked his glance down only at the first lines. "A half a barrel of tap beer. Fah! This we already know."

So they'd finally got the telephone bugged. That was nice to know. "Some of those things I ordered over the telephone, Mr. Farber. Most of them I've got to research before I can do anything more," and he picked up the carbon again to scan it more carefully.

"A jet airplane." Farber snorted. "Complete with stewardess and bar?"

Deadpan, I said, "A British 4-18, medium-range, fifty-five passenger capacity reduced and fitted for sixteen executives, bar and long-range fuel tanks installed, ninety-day delivery from today, flight and maintenance tutelage provided for one year, price seventeen million three hundred dollars cash. I have it in English pounds if you want."

Sawyer, of Commerce, made a long face. There were at least two air-frame builders in the United States that would have liked that order and the publicity that went with it. Farber looked up from his carbon copy and Mac was still studying his, to the open envy of Sawyer and Bolio who were sitting next to him.

Farber, in almost a whine: "Dictionaries, maps, atlases, encyclopedias, those we can understand. . . . Art?" he muttered peevishly. "What's he mean by 'art'? Or photographs . . . these should be listed with encyclopedias and dictionaries," indignantly.

"These," I reminded him, "are just the way he

dictated them. Not exactly dictated; he was just thinking out loud."

He went on down the list, pursing his lips and mumbling. "A detective agency to find out about things? What things?"

I saw Bolio of the FBI brighten. Now maybe *he'd* have a chance to carry the ball.

I hated to take away his helmet when I said, "Ken Jordan has already picked out his detective agency: Burns is outside his door and he likes the way they work." This wasn't credit-card true, but the Burns guard who was Jimbo's brother-in-law had gotten me in to Jordan and I owed Burns a favor even if Farber didn't know it. And don't think I didn't feel the grin behind Mac's stolid mask.

"Oh, good God in heaven!" Farber's wail of real agony was unashamed and at once he had everyone's eye. Mac, more practical and quick to realize he had missed something on the carbon copy list, started back over what he had read.

Farber's voice was scratchy when he read aloud. "Listen to this! 'A list of all the countries in the world that have no restrictions on the purchase, possession, or resale of gold or other precious metals.' "

This seemed to impress only one of the unintroduced men and Sawyer, who both seemed to react as though they had been hit. Mac, my boss, frowned as he tried to make some connection. Farber dropped the carbon on the motel end table, got up abruptly, and said, "Will you excuse me for one minute, perhaps two?" He went to the bar that comes with every salesman's suite and squirted himself a glass of plain seltzer. For at least three minutes he stood there finishing the water while the rest of us appreciated the drama, and then he came back with his prohibitionist Maine mind made up to a portentous decision.

"Mrs. Iverson," he said in his clipped nasal bark, "without permission I am going to supply several reasons why you are at the present time absolutely essential to your country. Some of us in this room know what I am going to tell you, some of us do not. I will not insult either their intelligence or mine by mentioning secrecy. What a few of us now know soon will be public knowledge.

"Very briefly, Mr. Jordan, while he was in Switzerland, made some type of deal, yet unknown, with the government of Switzerland. Through our various sources, we have found out that at a Swiss military airport Mr. Jordan's 'admiral's barge,' his spacecraft, landed some type of cargo. A great deal of cargo. We are not certain of its exact composition, as yet."

From an inside pocket he brought out a paper and referred to it as he went on. "This cargo consisted of from two hundred and fifty to three hundred squarish blocks of unknown material approximately two feet in each dimension. This in itself means nothing, and only a fortunate incident made it possible to determine that each of these blocks—in a cube only two feet square, mind you—weighs at least several tons." He looked for a reaction, found none from me, and went to squirt another glass of seltzer before he continued.

"We are facing an alien psychology, gentlemen—and Mrs. Iverson, of course—and we must make the inevitable inferences and deductions. Mr. Jordan's Captain Lee Lukkari stated that the Regan Group would supply, if I remember rightly, 'suitable means of exchange.'

"Now we must move to theory and mathematics. There are very few substances that weigh five tons that can be compressed into a two-foot cube. These are unique, quite rare, and valuable for certain purposes: platinum, osmium, iridium . . . and gold.

"Gold," as he went to his paper, "weighs some 1,905 pounds per cubic foot; two cubic feet multiplies everything by eight, and would weigh quite close to ten thousand pounds, five tons. Have you any idea of what one cubic foot of gold would be worth, at the present rate of exchange of the government of the United States, Mrs. Iverson?"

No, I hadn't thought of it. I'd thrown my gold-plated wedding ring down the toilet.

"An unbelievable figure, Mrs. Iverson and gentlemen. Quite fantastic! One block of gold one foot square would be worth—" He consulted the paper again— "There seems to be some confusion here comparing troy and avoirdupois weight, whatever those are—but at sixteen ounces to our pound this nugget of gold would be worth some $674,800, payable promptly upon demand at any United States mint. Multiply this one-foot cube by eight and the value soars to $780,249,600. A complication here; get the gold outside our national borders and many nations will pay from their stocks of our American dollars, or in their own coinage, as high as fifty dollars per ounce. You grasp these figures? Now, note that I stated that up to three hundred of these blocks are now stored in Swiss government vaults; some, we have reason to believe, are of the heavier metals and are of such greater value as to make dollars and cents almost astronomical. For osmium, at the present market, over six billion dollars."

I gave up trying to estimate the total value of Ken Jordan's cargo. Mac, of course, had tipped me off about the Swiss lode, although where he got his first inside information I would probably never know.

Farber teetered on his heels. "Our deductions lead

us, gentlemen, to a very solid conclusion: that the government of the United States—and quite possibly every other government that bases its coinage on the gold standard, which means the world—is in severe trouble. Will Mr. Jordan sell his gold to Washington for thirty-five American dollars per ounce when he can get fifty dollars per ounce from Delhi or Paris or Moscow? Particularly Moscow!"

To myself, I thought, *So we pay a hundred dollars an ounce,* but Farber was a jump ahead of me.

"Let's simplify it, gentlemen. Instead of dollars let us say loaves of bread, which is what, basically, our dollars represent. If we can offer only two loaves of bread and some other nation three loaves, who loses out? The low bidder, obviously."

I had a question. "Mr. Farber, instead of paying only thirty-five dollars an ounce, why can't we pay fifty dollars an ounce, or whatever anyone else pays? Aren't we supposed to be the richest nation in the world? Or am I just so stupid that I don't get the point?"

No, I wasn't stupid, but his tone made it clear that he thought I was. "Not at all, Mrs. Iverson, not at all. What you have missed is the small detail that our government has based its economy on paying only thirty-five dollars per ounce for gold. This is our law, and it is illegal to sell gold at any other figure."

On Main Street it's illegal, but on Threadneedle Street and the Champs Elysées it's good business. I should have known better than to ask a question. Ever try to tell any Establishment man, from flatfoot to railroad dick, that the law is wrong?

Farber shook himself out of his American Eden where no one could buy gold at more than thirty-five dollars per ounce. "Now, you have the facts, Mrs. Iverson, as we ourselves know them, as scanty as are our deductions and as faulty as may be our basic information." He brooded about that, too, before he went on. "Another item of peculiar interest—I might say vital and special interest—to the Department of Defense, a pleasing euphemism to soothe the spartan soul," he added distastefully.

"Our military cohorts are extremely, frantically interested in a vehicle that lifts not only itself but (allowing five tons for each part of a three hundred-piece cargo) some fifteen hundred tons' payload silently and effortlessly to a height and/or range quite beyond our utmost technical ability. Our Space Administration Group mourns in stunned silence, gentlemen and Mrs. Iverson, but the brotherhood of the shiny brass insignia is much more vocal in its demands for technical details lest another nation, quite possibly unfriendly, with foreign-garbed and similarly minded myrmidons, find out what's in Pandora's levitating box before we do." Frowning: "Visualize the forthcoming need for close coordination.

"You, Mrs. Iverson, may, and I hope, will be our ace in the hole, if you'll pardon the colloquialism." Turning to Mac: "Mr. McLeod, you will forward Mrs. Iverson's 201 file and all her pertinent information to me personally in Washington. Clear channels will be immediately set up for procedures down the line to Mrs. Iverson—"

"Mr. Farber," I broke in. Mac had gone to bat for me in the past and my memory is good. "Mr. Farber, does this mean I'll be working for you instead of Mr. McLeod?"

Farber beamed. "Of course, of course. And," he added silkily, "I wouldn't be surprised if there might not be a step-in-grade promotion at a later date."

"No."

He misunderstood. "Oh, not very long, Mrs. Iverson.

Not long at all. We keep staff happy in our Department of State."

"No, Mr. Farber."

A dead stop in his thinking. "No, Mrs. Iverson?"

"No, Mr. Farber. I've worked for Mr. McLeod for five—almost six years. He approved hiring me as a GS-4; approved two quality commendations, two step-in-grades, and I'm now a GS-9, the only female field operative in the section." I looked straight at Waldron, Mac's boss, who reddened. "I didn't ever expect to make GS-9; it happened when someone was off on annual leave." Women are supposed to be bitches, aren't they?

Farber was stunned. People don't talk back to high echelons.

"I'm sorry, Mr. Farber. I like working for Mr. McLeod. I work for him; I report to him." And I threw the bungstarter: "Or I could transfer, let's say, to Internal Revenue."

There was a long, long pause. There was quirking at the corners of Bolio's mouth, the FBI resident agent. Waldron, Mac's boss, was sullen brick red at the remark I had made. Sawyer, the Commerce man, was eyeing me with wonder that anyone would say no to Farber. And Mac? He hadn't moved a muscle in his body or his face when I had laid it on the line for him. But I knew if ever any man belonged to any woman, body and mind, for a few minutes it was McLeod, that ugly, ornery old scoundrel. And both of us knew that if I lost my importance and the job with Ken Jordan, we had collected deadly permanent enemies from top to bottom in any branch of Federal service, deadly enough jobwise to make us . . . Oh, well.

Farber's clockwork ticked. Grudgingly, after a curious appraisal of Mac and myself to determine who might have been sleeping with whom and deciding the possibility was remote, he said, "We bow to the man-on-the-spot, Mrs. Iverson. You will continue to report to Mr. McLeod," and it was so good to see how the old buzzard handled it.

Without changing position Mac seemed to stand tall. "Thank you, Iverson. That will be all for tonight. Keep in touch."

I nodded, gathered my purse, and stood up. "Thank you, Mr. McLeod, good night, gentlemen," and I left. I took my time closing the door and held it open the last fraction of an inch to hear Farber say with almost vicious vocal snap, "I think that will be all for tonight, gentlemen. Mr. McLeod, would it be possible that you might stay a few extra minutes—" Waldron was out—Mac was in. I let the door close.

Tomorrow I had to get up early to go to work for Ken Jordan and the Regan Group.

## Chapter Eight

Ken Jordan was still not in his suite when I reported for work the next morning. As I started the old Detroit routine of leaving my car parked in front of my house and walking to Harper to catch the express bus downtown, I felt as though I had been working for him for a long time. Since I knew my own neighborhood and knew that on my narrow street every homeowner—if they valued their quarter-panels—parked in their driveway or garage, it was with some interest that I noted a black Chevrolet parked at the corner. I took the long way around the block to satisfy myself that it was one of Bolio's men. I was right, and when I walked past he ignored me and I him, although we had met before. It was a nice feeling to know I had coverage, as I suspected that eventually, on this job, I would need it. I read the *Free Press* on the bus to work and enjoyed the conjectures about Ken Jordan and his "heavily guarded mystery suite," knowing that I was the "sultry disembodied feminine voice that refused all entrance and that, for this curious reporter, had no comment."

A Statler assistant manager soloed me to the sixteenth floor (as indeed someone did all the rest of the time of our stay at the hotel; no elevators were allowed to stop at our floor without a previous clearance from Jordan or myself) with a great box of mail that had accumulated almost overnight. The Burns guard toted the box inside for me; Jordan's bedroom door was open with the beds unrumpled. "Tomcat," I thought as I went to work with the telephone. I knocked off for lunch, then went back to slaving, and, about two in the afternoon, with most of Jordan's requested information either in hand, in process, or on the way, started slitting open the mail. Some of it was out-and-out crank junk, but most of it was pure business. And very important business, at that. The thick bond paper, the engraved letterheads from some of the largest corporations in the country (the foreign mail started coming in two days later), and the signatures suddenly stressed for me just how really important this Jordan was. The telegrams, of which there were almost many as letters, were from Europeans, Asiatics, and Africans. Most astonishing of all were the three personal cablegrams from heads of states.

I made a list of the ones I thought Jordan should read or at least know about and started through the file of telephone slips. Of these there weren't many, because Jordan was accepting no calls unless they were important enough to terrify the assistant manager. I had informed Statler personnel twice already that maybe Time, Inc., and the Detroit newspapers might impress them, but Jordan would talk to no one, and that meant me, too, unless the place was on fire. In the pile of slips; a polite note from Secretary Ngambi of the United Nations consisting of formal greetings from the UN to the Ambassador of the Regan Group, personal regards from Ngambi, and words to the effect that, with the whole world waiting, would Mr. Jordan accept his official invitation to visit and discuss various matters on the United Nations floor?

There were three separate slips from Farber, the Department of State man from the meeting last night, who apparently, judging by the wording on the three notes, had become increasingly desperate. There was a note from the Statler tabulating the total calls, which ran into a ridiculous figure, and asking if the hotel service was satisfactory at all times. That led me to look at my watch, estimate my hunger, and decide to call it a day. It was now almost dark outside.

The telephone rang while I was in the bathroom. It was Jordan's voice from Ottawa, Canada.

"Hi, babe," he said cheerfully. "Whaddya doing there so late—working or drinking my booze?"

"Neither," I told him. "I was just getting ready to leave, Mr. Jordan—I mean Ken Jordan."

"Glad I caught you," he said. "Something just dawned on me when I wanted to buy the house a drink and I didn't have enough money. You got money?"

"Well," I said, mentally going through my purse, "about—"

"That's what I thought," he said. "You're broke too. I went off and left you without cash in the till. I didn't even think about it until I sneaked out of the meeting I'm in to get something besides this weak Canadian whiskey. I like something that you can taste. Got your pencil? OK. Now call the Swiss Embassy in Washington and ask for Herr Schillmoeller," and he spelled it out for me. "Tell him he should send me some money now and you take what you need till I get back."

"I can get along." I was touched that he had been thinking of my poverty between drinks.

"Oh, sure," he said roughly. "Two bucks in your pocket and bean soup in the icebox. Take what you want and I'll see you later."

"Wait a minute," I said quickly. "When is that? The operator said you were in Ottawa."

"Oh, maybe a day or so. I'm trying to buy myself an island. Keep the store open, kid, and watch the shoplifters," and he hung up.

I looked at the clock, said the hell with it, and mixed myself a nice big martini from Jordan's well-equipped bar. Then, with the drink at my elbow and feeling like a cross between Dorothy of Oz and Maid Marian, I called the Swiss embassy.

Herr Schillmoeller's first name was Wolff, and he had a youthful breezy American accent. I identified myself, repeated Jordan's instructions, and waited.

"Of course—is that Miss or Mrs. Dana Iverson?"

"Neither one," I said. "Just Dana Iverson. And it's just Ken Jordan, no Mister. That seems to be the setup here."

"Of course," he repeated. "Here in Washington we have been fully informed. Which bank would you prefer?"

This I hadn't thought about, and I hesitated. Then I remembered suddenly what Farber, State Department, had said about foreign gold and I played a hunch. It turned out later that it was so exactly what Jordan had wanted and had forgotten to tell me that he gradually grew convinced that he had told me after all.

"How about the Bank of Montreal in Windsor?" I suggested. I'd seen the bank's sign many times when my disgustingly-few dates had taken me to Windsor for smorgasbord at Gan's.

No question. The Bank of Montreal was my choice, and Wolff Schillmoeller would be there at the start of banking hours. Had I already made arrangements with the staff of the Bank of Montreal?

No, I hadn't.

"Of course, Dana Iverson. Merely detail? Shall we meet tomorrow, perhaps?"

This Wolff sounded nicely wolfish. "Perhaps, Herr Schillmoeller . . . Wait a minute. Did you say tomorrow, in Windsor?"

"But of course. Such a sum of money, even between governments, requires a certain amount of paperwork and personal liaison. I shall leave immediately. By air it is only a very short trip, and plans have been laid for this very eventuality." Hopefully he added, "If Dana Iverson might not mind a latish dinner, the government of Switzerland and myself personally would be honored and I would even more eagerly speed our modern Swissair jet. . . ."

Not on your life, Wolfie. I never had a blind date in my life that wasn't a bore. I made excuses, then: "You said 'such a sum of money,' Herr Schillmoeller. What would you say it would add up to?"

Wolfie's voice, with the European-designed sentences and the American accent, grew reverent. "For the resources of the Regan Group, not a great deal, but for a small government such as ours a princely sum. Ken Jordan mentioned no figure, I believe, but our instructions from Geneva were to be prepared for increments of logical size."

"How much?" I said again.

"With your approval, of course, I shall arrange the transferral of four hundred millions of Swiss francs."

Francs? That was different. I once bought a hot camera in Palermo only because I liked paying a hundred thousand lire out all at once. "How much would that be in American dollars, Herr Schillmoeller?"

He was ready with the answer. "Just divide by four, Dana Iverson, and shift the decimal point. This would be, at the present rate of exchange" (and I thought he emphasized "present rate") "about one hundred million, three hundred and twenty thousand American dollars."

"Dollars?" I repeated. "Dollars?"

"Dollars. American dollars. I say, are you there?"

"Yes," I admitted weakly. "I'm here. Thank you very much, Herr Schillmoeller. I just don't feel very well. No, just temporary. Good night, and thank you again; I'm going right home to bed." And, believe me, I did.

This, when I come to think about it, might be the real beginning of Ken Jordan's story, and mine.

Jordan took two afternoons to show up. He had bought his island. He sheepishly entered his suite carrying a painter's roller, a paint-spattered pail, and a defiant look.

"All right," he said, "all *right!* Even the cab driver recognized the doctor clothes and I had to switch cabs, make a deal with the first painter I saw, and come up the freight elevator. So where's that tap beer you were going to get?" He spotted it before I could tell him, expertly drew off a big mug, and gulped a huge glug. "Not as good as Canadian beer. You can't taste their whiskey, though. What's new, kid?"

I said, "I hoped you'd tell me."

He drank the rest of his stein, refilled, lolled crosswise in the biggest chair, and told me what he had been doing.

He'd sold the Mayor of Windsor, gone directly in the mayor's car to Toronto to see the Windsor riding representatives (the equivalent of United States state officials), and ended up in Ottawa, Canada's capital. And he'd bought outright, with no strings, no reservations, Peche Island.

(Peche Island is at the head of the Detroit River, lying entirely within Ontario. Almost exactly one mile long and one half mile wide, it had been first a summer home for Canada's biggest distiller, then a comfortably deserted rendezvous for amorous couples with a boat [I remember my dad and mother giggling about the mythical "glass house" he had taken her to see], and finally, after an abortive attempt to turn it into a private amusement park, it had deteriorated into a weedy woody tract regarded as a liability alike by the City of Windsor and the province.)

"You bought an island?"

"Uh-uh," he corrected. "The Regan Group bought it. Know what I paid for it?" He watched my reaction. "Thirty million dollars. Ten million to Canada, ten to Ontario, and ten million to the City of Windsor. They're still arguing in Ottawa," as he hefted his beer glass. "But the deal is solid. . . . You don't think thirty million bucks is a lot of money?"

I smiled at him. "Mr. Jord—Ken Jordan, the Swiss government deposited over one hundred million dollars in the Bank of Montreal for you; with that figure in mind . . . well, now everything is relative. And there are papers for you to sign. The Bank of Montreal, after recovering from the shock, is holding the Swiss transfer like a hot porcupine."

There was some discussion about procedures and it ended with a popeyed Bank of Montreal representative racing from Windsor with a notary to witness signatures. When the afternoon was over, I—as easily as Jordan—could sign any check for any amount on the Regan Group account for any reason at any time. I thought he was insane, and said so.

"Look, Iverson," he said patiently. "This is just peanuts compared to what I got stashed in Switzerland. How far do you think you'd get if you cleaned the till and took off, and I doubled what you lift to catch up with you? That's number one. Besides, I gotta have somebody to keep track, or sign, or pay things when I'm not around. Three, in every shop I ever worked where you had to sign for reamers and stuff because they were afraid you'd steal them, they got stolen. If you figure you're going to get taken, you will. You seem to know the score, and this is going to be a pretty good job. Why ruin it? Say, we never talked money! How much did you make on the last job you had?"

I gave him my present GS-9 income. "That was every other Thursday, less deductions."

He grinned, altering his facial lines from a soak to a beery pixie, and he told me my new salary.

I looked at him. "Every month?"

"Ha!" he said. "I had a job once where I got paid on the fifth of the month. From the fifth to the twenty-fifth I was drinking the best; then up to the fifth of next month I was cadging nickel beers. Nope, payday every Thursday."

I swung around and faced him squarely. "This job, Ken Jordan, this job, no office job is worth that much. What's the pitch?"

"No pitch," and he thought it over. "I guess you know that I got Lee Lukkari in my head?"

"Have you, really?" I found it hard to believe.

"Yeah. Really." He stared at his beer and put it on the end table to walk over to the window. He continued to talk and as he went on it began to dawn on me that he didn't want to look me in the face.

"Sure have," he said slowly. "I've got everything she knows and everything she ever did, and she's got everything of mine squeezed into her head. If I had known what she was going to do I wouldn't have gone through with it—hell, I can always make a living working a machine. She knew it, she told me after, but it was too late, and she knew that, too. Come to think of it, it must have been rugged on her, too, having some stranger know everything she ever did or thought of. Say!" eagerly, "I never knew that women—" Even at that distance I saw him flush and he never finished his sentence. With his back solidly toward me he finished with, "Well, you know what I mean."

"Anyway, maybe she did get the dirty end of the stick. She'll spend the rest of her life studying the stuff I send, making lists and interpreting, cataloguing and translating, stuff like that."

I slid in a casual question. "How did she change minds with you?"

"Nah," he said absently. "No swap, just squeezing both of us in the same skull. You mean how she did it? I sure don't know, Iverson. I remember waking in the lifeboat—that's what it is, you know—passing out cold and understanding her funny-like when I waked up. It took me a while to figure out that now I knew a language I never knew before. When we traded *its* (or something that sounded like that), we just sat down together, but this time I felt lousy when I woke up, like getting lost in a hall of mirrors. I was even seeing double and doing things like reaching for something and missing it. It took us both almost a couple of weeks to get that sorted out.

"The worst was sleeping. I'd wake up yelling or crying like a baby and they'd slip me some kind of a mickey to go back to sleep and wake up again and get another drink. And all the time I knew she was getting the same bad dreams as I did, for the same reasons. She told me later that she had been specially trained all her life for this transfer, and yet she still almost cracked up. If she did, the whole thing would have had to be done all over, because I couldn't take it again and she'd be out of the picture."

"Why?" I asked.

"Funny," he said. "A funny reason, to me, anyway. I've got her personality only so I could see or taste or feel or hear something and know that if she liked it the Regan Group would want it, or enough of it to make it profitable. Without both of us knowing, everything could be just like a slot machine with the buttons taped over."

"Profitable?" I said curiously. "This is all for money?"

Jordan shrugged and came back to sit down, a little tiredly, I thought. "No. Not dollar bills. But she works and now so do I for a Regan Group department that has to take in what the budget puts out. It's all going for research, but it's got to pay for itself. Let's say DuPont spends a fortune finding out how to make nylon, like they did years ago. Once they get off the nut—that's the R & D, the tooling—the patent goes public. Whatever else DuPont learns along the way is gravy."

I pushed my luck a little further. "What does the Regan Group want? What are the Regans like?"

He took a sip of his almost empty jug and put it down firmly. "Trouble with swapping heads," he said sourly, "is that I like the hard stuff as much as I ever did, but Lee Lukkari gets a hangover. What are the others like, at least the ones I met? What do we want?"

*We want.* It was the first time he had identified himself as part of the "we."

"Lots of things," he said. "Some of them you should have by now. Right?"

"Right. Or on the way."

"Some things, when I think of them, Lee Lukkari's head in my head says yes; the rest, I know will come up later. If they don't, she'll get in touch with me. She'll be around for some time, because we'll need each other for quite a while. As to why, I'm not really sure, but I think I know. And as far as what the rest of us are like—" He was becoming more Regan by the word— "Lee Lukkari doesn't think you should know, and neither do I. Hey!"

I looked up, startled.

"Where's your Regan clothes? And my pants and shirt?"

I explained that they were ready, waiting for his fitting. Tomorrow morning?

A glance at the clock. "That late already? OK. You order me plenty of spares. You know, even if all you have to do is dip them in water it's still a pain; Lee Lukkari wears nylons, once in a while; she washes them like you do." Back came his old Detroit leer, and I felt my face getting pink. "And, while I think of it, don't take me wrong, kid, but I got a whole floor, and we're gonna be here I don't know how long. Do you wanna get your rent free? Move in here someplace? I'm paying for it, and there's no use of these rooms going to waste." At once he realized what he had proposed, and the idiot almost shuffled his feet sitting down. "Aw, hell."

Very businesslike I was. "Well, thank you, Ken Jordan. I was wondering about that," and his mouth opened in surprise. "I must confess I've been the object of much curiosity since I started working for you, and some annoyance where I live." This was true. One enterprising European accent had been waiting for me in my living room the previous night, leaving abruptly when I picked up the telephone to ask for the police, and I'd had to leave my telephone off the hook.

"I appreciate your housing offer—it is just a *housing* offer?"

He saw the smile I was wearing. "Yes, you knew it all the time. Pick out the place you want and move in. Hey, take one of these Burns guards with you to carry stuff. It's about time they did something besides standing around to earn their money."

By midnight the muttering uniformed guard had carried in the last sheaf of dress hangers and shoved the heavy hotel furniture to where I wanted it, I had made a long telephone call to Mac, my boss, I'd eaten a bacon and tomato sandwich from room service (if you tell them to leave out the lettuce you get more bacon), and I was uncomfortable in my new bed. It was quite a while before I slept.

# Chapter Nine

Jordan had a glorious time with his island while the economic cauldron from which he had pried the lid continued to spew forth nothing but difficulties—at least from my government's point of view.

Within ten days after the Canadian parliament OK'd his purchase of his island—amid stuffy mutterings from upper Ontario, Prince Rupert, and Moose Jaw that seeped through Ottawa—there was a landscaping crew at work. I bought two small Russian hovercrafts and a flotilla of barges with rented tugs for haulage, leased enough generators to light a small city, and in seven months three-shift, seven-day crews had planed and shaped the island, dug and refilled holes, rafted material from the CNR docks in Windsor and C & O in Detroit, paid half a million dollars for Canadian Riverside Drive parking space and another ninety thousand for a hovercraft dock, arranged for Windsor water, telephone, and power from Ontario Hydro, and moved in.

There should be a long story in how much I went through by doing almost all of this myself, with only temporary Kelly girls at *my* bidding, for a change. In spite of Jordan's flat order that I should do no overtime work—and "if you need help, damn it, go hire it!"— I ended up by making mental notes of what to do tomorrow when I should have been asleep. Really, when I stop to think of it, it was not as insane as it sounds; I did no checking, no overseeing, just made statements of purchase or intent into a tape recorder, let the contracts, and went on to the next item. There always seemed to be another item chasing the last one. Jordan refused to sign anything; he said, "Regans put it on tape," and this naturally made it easy for me to make duplicates for my real boss, the United States government. Mac, my fearless leader, knew what was on Jordan's schedule as soon as I did. Looking back, it was a frantic and sometimes angry period, but it was then I first fully understood how easy it is to buy quality, to get things done if you can pay cash or have unlimited credit. So in seven months we moved onto Peche Island, with a tiny office and Jordan's temporary living quarters—both vacant—spotted attractively around the landscape. One thing that puzzled me—and my government bosses—was that flatboats were still operating piledrivers around the island's perimeter.

While all this was going on, with a heartful of innocence Jordan played merry hell with everything.

He had appeared in the United Nations with Secretary Ngambi, who, I suspect, was healthily glad that his term as secretary was due to expire. Jordan, now sure of his financial standing and new social position, sat easily in front of the assembly and told the world that, no, he knew nothing about this diplomatic stuff and as far as he was concerned he didn't intend to learn. He was a purchasing agent, and if anyone wanted to sell what he wanted to buy—OK.

Everyone by now knew of his Swiss cache; only it wasn't all gold. It included tungsten, rhodium, palladium, osmium, platinum, and practically everything that weighed heavily in a small space. (Later, after things got rolling, he sold the other metals to whoever wanted to trade for Swiss francs; he kept the gold for his own account, using the Swiss francs and the Swiss government as his exchange agents. Almost everyone, including industries who began to find new uses for the now plentiful heavy metals, was happy. Almost everyone.)

The United States ambassador got the floor. "Mr. Jordan. I understand you intend to buy various items."

Jordan nodded. "Or materials."

"Or materials, Mr. Jordan. Thank you. Could you tell us what items or materials?"

A shrug from Jordan. He was probably thirsty. "I don't know yet. I've got to set up a system before I make up my mind."

The ambassador said, "Mr. Jordan, we shall be awaiting with great interest your considered decisions. Speaking as the representative of one of the world's great industrial nations . . ." The ambassador scooted off that tack in a big hurry when his sales pitch backfired, to impolite growls from the assembly. Changing back to second gear he said hurriedly, "I'm sure, Mr. Jordan, you're familiar with the fact that national laws vary. You will purchase these 'items and materials' through the government of Switzerland, another great industrial nation?"

Jordan looked surprised. "Why should I? The gold in Switzerland is being stored for me. What I buy, I pay for in cash."

The American pounced on that. "Cash, Mr. Jordan? Gold is a metal; we can hardly call it cash."

It didn't impress Jordan. "You can't, maybe, but I can. For years now you've been claiming you're on a gold standard. So I have gold. You say your dollar bills are based on gold, the Swiss francs are based on gold, and you haven't got that much gold. I have. So I'll pay in cash. No paper money with pretty pictures, but the real thing: gold. Cash on delivery."

The American took a deep breath. "Yes, Mr. Jordan—"

Jordan said sourly, "Why not forget I used to be *Mr.* Jordan, except when a cop stopped me? The Regan Group—well, the name is Ken Jordan. Forget the Mister."

A polite bow. "I stand corrected, Ken Jordan. But to return: it is not customary, as you realize, to make the actual transfer of a metal with any transaction—"

Jordan grinned. "No? I got a few old silver dollars stashed away."

This was ignored. "And in some places the physical possession of certain metals is actually illegal."

Jordan shook his head positively. "Not where I come from—I mean, not where I belong. If I buy anything, I pay cash on the beerkeg. You sell, I buy, I pay. On the spot. With gold."

The ambassador raised his eyebrows. "Delivery and payment in Switzerland, halfway across the world?"

There was a pause while Jordan casually flicked his glance around the room. "No. Delivery *and* payment at the nearest Regan Group outpost, formerly known as Peche Island, transferred irrevocably to our group by the sovereign state of Canada." I remember he had made me pronounce "irrevocably" three times.

He added thoughtfully, "The Swiss government now stores the assets of the Regan Group until" (and it sounded as though he had memorized the speech) "our Regan Group outpost is completed. Then Regan Group assets will be transferred to our own territory."

At once I thought how quick a Mafia raid or commando strike would hit once billions of dollars of gold landed on a mile-long beach of a dimestore island in the middle of a heavily trafficked river.

The American ambassador opened his mouth, but Jordan wasn't finished.

"There might be some worry about the proper care for such a large amount of—say, ready cash. But such worry would be needless," and his smirk was a foot wide. "The ready cash, or means of exchange, will be perfectly safe. Our Regan Group will see to that."

The United States representative made a final effort. "Mr.—Ken Jordan, it is illegal, for example, for a United States citizen or group to even possess gold. It has been a statutory offense for some time. Let us suppose that some one person or group has 'items or material' the Regan Group desires to purchase. The illegality of possessing—"

He was waved away almost petulantly. "If they have it, if I want it, if they deliver it, I pay for it on my doorstep. As far as being illegal, that's your group's laws." He sat up and stretched. "It's also illegal to sell dirty pictures, but they get made, sold, and bought. Don't tell me how to spend my own money." The American sat down to pick up his desk communicator, with which he argued for the rest of the assembly.

The assembly, like the rest of the world, was interested in almost equal amounts in what's in it for us and how about more data on the Regan Group? No one got any more definite answer to the first proposition than had the United States representative. To the second, Jordan was slightly more informative.

He told them very little. He was to be their sole contact with the Regan Group, and Captain Lukkari would be available if necessary.

Where was Captain Lukkari right now?

"Resting, maybe. Certainly combining her new knowledge with her own."

They pounced. Was it really true that Jordan and the woman captain had exchanged brains?

"Hell, no. She just knows everything I know and vice versa. Any funny ideas you get are probably right. On top of that, I still don't know what I know until I stop to think about it. It gets very complicated."

Would Ken Jordan tell how all this was done?

He repeated what he had already told me. He admitted at once that the actual technique he knew nothing about, and neither did his Captain Lukkari. It was highly specialized, quite difficult, required long training for a mind to accept deliberate subordination—

Deliberate?

"Sure. Right now Lee Lukkari thinks a lot more like me than I do like her. This is so the Regan Group can't consciously overrride or ignore the way I used to think—the way any Earth Group person thinks. It's got to come through loud and clear, not the way they might expect to hear from some hired hand."

Why had Jordan been chosen as the first contact?

He brooded the question. "I dunno exactly. . . . Yes, I do. It's because back in history—our Regan Group—even the best experts made so many mistakes it was decided that a random choice that could very well start out with the worst possible poker hands being dealt accepted all the difficulties right at the very beginning; this is the time when mistakes get the most attention."

And if the cruiser KAYTA had picked its first contact from African jungles or from the Australian back bush?

Jordan shrugged that away. "Not the way we

work." He was using the Regan "we" again. "We look for settlements of individuals, collections of industry—parks are very important—conditions of home and living, broadcasts and telecasts and the content of the programs" (lucky they couldn't understand the U.S. TV commercials) "and other things. But again it's a random choice from a set of areas with roughly equal traits. So it was Detroit and Ken Jordan. It could just as easily have been Chicago or Cleveland, just to name two."

Why not New York?

"Too big. Too many people."

Why not London?

"Same thing, plus *surrounded* by water. Affects the thinking, not good, not bad, just affects it."

Then why not Moscow?

"Too far from water. Too cold too long."

Why not San Francisco? Why not Odessa?

"San Francisco was one of the possibilities. Odessa? I don't know much about cities anywhere except the U.S.A. If I had a map I could point it out, or any other city that got fed into the choicemaker—well, why should I? I just happened to be at the right place at the right time."

A husky man stood up in the Russian delegation.

"Could you tell, please, how long it was pondered before a firm decision was made by the Regan Group?"

Jordan studied the Slav before he answered. "In other words, you really want to know how long we have been checking Earth?" He cocked his head, scratched his nose, and counted on his fingers rather apologetically. "Takes me a little time to get this figured out in my head. . . . About . . . about twenty-one years, give or take a few months."

The Russian howled. "Ha! Ha, Ken Jordan! You say

twenty-one years, and yet we have firm, yes, positive evidence, that your flying saucers have been observing my nation, violating our airspace and our integrity, for much longer than twenty-one years, even back beyond the People's War Against Fascism. This, Ken Jordan, you can perhaps explain?" He sat down and made triumphant noises.

Slowly Jordan shook his head. "No, I can't explain it. The cruiser KAYTA has never been within—within a great distance from Earth. You saw our landing ship—neither that nor the cruiser KAYTA looks anything like a flying saucer. But I'm interested. I can't explain it, but I'm interested."

The Russian snorted, disbelieving, and sat back in his chair with his arms folded.

Jordan closed the conference with a whispered request to Secretary Ngambi, who got up to say the right words, and it ended with Jordan heading, certainly, for the bar with the standing assembly applauding more or less enthusiastically when Jordan agreed to appear again in a month.

Back on Peche Island, I turned off the TV, turned on the FM, picked up the telephone, and went back to work.

# Chapter Ten

Jordan flew back to the island, picking up on the way his British jet at Newark, landing in solitary style at the Windsor airport. This he told me over a mug of Canadian ale after he strolled in and caught me working.

"I hired myself two pilots," he said hopefully. "Both young fellows. Well, maybe one, anyway. The other one is engaged in Manchester and wants to think it over. Hire them in, hey?"

"Right away," I said courteously. "Not that I know their names or their salary, or how much they're going to earn. How about setting up some kind of bookkeeping system, for example? Not right away, but about two years from now when I've cleaned up all this stuff on the desk?"

"Why not?" Jordan said happily. "You're running the joint. Want a beer?"

I snapped at him. "Now look here, Ken Jordan! While you've been hogging the camera I've been up to my kilts in work—"

"Nice kilts, too."

"And it's about time you sat down and set up some kind of a system for everything. Do you realize—"

"Sure," he said. "Calm down. I've been doing some thinking about the whole thing. . . . Don't do anything yourself, or you can if you want to drive yourself crazy, but you can't get paid for that. Set up some kind of employment office someplace on shore" (he was already talking like a naval seigneur) "and then—"

"And then hire four million watchmen to guard this island, each equipped with waterwings and howitzers. Are you really going to move all your gold right here?"

He nodded. "In about a month. Can you have everything laid out by then? Who we want to hire and so on?"

Who *we* wanted to hire. It made me part of the family, did it? "Who *do* we want to hire?"

He didn't know. "You managed a small office, now manage a big one." He went on after he finished his mug. "What you don't know, find out. Find someone, pick his brains, and make *him* to do all the work. Check with me if you're in doubt, but you can handle it. First thing, call Burns and hire some more guards. Keep everyone off the island, but no guns. Pound hell out of snoopers if they're persistent, but no guns."

"And you're going to protect billions of dollars with nightsticks and a bunch of creaky retired cops?"

His grin meant he didn't. Well, I'd find out. He said, "Hell, no. Not with guards. . . . Say, if you're so busy, how come those two phones aren't ringing?"

"We have two lines from the Windsor exchange to here: the second, which cost nothing, and the first, which cost seventy-one thousand dollars for repair of the underwater cable and a backup microtower, and they're both shut off so I can get things done. Any other questions?"

"Jeez," he said, "you do know all the answers. Try another one: you still living at the hotel?"

"Where else, with free rent?"

"Right here, with everyone else that you hire."

"In tents, on cots, with oildrum showers and picnic tables?"

"Nope. A hall, sort of."

"Barracks!"

"A hall for the single ones, homes or apartments for married ones."

"Like what?"

"Like the kind they want, like the architect will design for them, and I pay the bills."

"Like who will want to live a mile from anywhere, under the boss's nose?"

"Young people, probably, or old pros who'll all make more money here than anyplace else. Big salaries, good pensions, long vacations . . ."

"Why, Ken Jordan? Why? Why lead someone's life for them by making him live on a one-mile piece of company town? Are you trying to go back five or six hundred years?" This I did not like.

"No," he said in an odd tone. "Just the opposite . . . I got reasons, kid, I got reasons."

I got hot inside and switched on the telephones to hide my annoyance. Both lines burst into life at once and he stood up and stretched. "Think it over, sugar; I got reasons," and he strolled out the office door.

They were good reasons, too, as I was to discover much later.

It took only one rumor, telephoned by myself to the Windsor *Star* and the Detroit *Free Press*, to flood our post office box even more thoroughly than ever before, and our augmented Burns guards were pressed to utmost ingenuity in keeping job-hunters off the shores of the island. The ones that got through, mostly at night despite the spotlights, got bounced when it became light enough to catch rabbits. It took three weeks, much investigating by Burns of the applicants' backgrounds, and plenty of juggling by various federal staffs before I brought over our two hovercrafts from Windsor loaded with the thirty-seven successful job-hunters. Twenty-four of them were federal plants, some of whom I had known personally at one time or another on past jobs. Ken Jordan was eager to greet them, bought drinks and had catered dinners shipped from Roumell's, circulated energetically most of the afternoon telling dirty stories to the men while staring at the women's legs, and hired not a single one.

That night Mac himself met me in a restaurant out Six Mile. He was furious.

"Somebody blew it," he said flatly. "Not to hire even one out of all the list . . . No, somebody blew the cover. This I'm just as certain of as that I'm sitting here. Didn't Jordan act in any way different?" and I shook my head. "No funny looks, no telephone calls on the sly?"

I looked at Mac disgustedly. He was tapped into our underwater cable and taped every call as fast it was made, and Mac knew I knew it.

"Nothing?" he insisted. "Damn that Jordan anyway, after all the trouble. . . . You don't think he was reading minds or something?"

"If he's read my mind we're already dead," I reminded him. "What's good for dessert?"

"Blueberry pie," he said. "Make it two?" as he waved at the waitress.

"Make it two. You found out about the piledrivers, I imagine."

"Yeah," he said. "How come nothing shows on the original blueprints you copied?" I shrugged. "Well, it's some kind of foundation in a perfect oval around the whole island, running down to bedrock, and that's quite a distance down in that soil, I understand."

"So?"

"So nothing," he said gloomily. "They're strong as all get-out and designed to take a big load, so big no one can figure out what they would carry."

A wall, my first thought.

"Mine, too, but the tech boys say not. And the top of the foundations happen to be just a little over nine inches below the lowest water level recorded since the Coast Guard's been interested."

"We'll find out. I can ask Jordan what those crews are still working on offshore, you know; they do make an ungodly thumping all day long."

"OK," he said absently. Then back to his original subject. "Jordan said nothing, gave no indication why he rejected the whole lot of applicants?"

I ran my mind back conscientiously. "Nothing. He just sat there after they left; he was beered up as usual, and said he didn't like the looks of any of them."

Mac almost snarled. "Their looks! He had at least four of the sexiest babes this side of any bedroom to pick from, and he didn't like their looks."

I cocked my head as a stray thought slid in. "Did you ever stop to think that, if he has a woman's mind alongside his own, he may not be interested in sexy babes anymore?"

Mac sat up and stared. "By God, I never thought of that!"

"Neither did I till just now," I said slowly. "You know, Mac, he's never made any kind of pass at me?"

He grinned as he remembered his own pass at me when I was still married and a lot dumber. "You got something, kid; that dog's not normal!" —which was a fair compliment, and I took it that way. "I want to think this out," which meant he'd check with the staff brains, "but what else did he say or do?"

I licked the pie fork clean. "He'll take over finding all the right people. He'll use the organization chart I made up—all right, the chart made up for me—and he'll do the hiring to save me the trouble."

"Snotty? Sarcastic?"

"Not one bit," I told him. "Nice as can be."

"Too nice?"

"No dice, Mac. Just sorry that I went to all that trouble and a little apologetic that he didn't like the crop I dug up."

The waitress came up to tell Mac he was wanted on the bar telephone. While he was gone I went to where I could do things like look in a decent mirror. Right, Jordan hadn't made one single pass, and I knew what I looked like. This was what had been nagging at me for a long time, a missing piece of the jigsaw. What were the rest of the pieces?

Mac had one ready for me at the table.

"You're *sure* Jordan didn't—"

"Mac, you heard me. I'm sure."

"I heard you. You remember the young Filipino with a U. of D. master's degree in Business Ad.? He's not Filipino; he's from Ceylon, and he's done at least two jobs for the Soviets. The tall redhead from Toronto?"

This one I had admired enough to go back and recheck his application after I'd seen him step off our hovercraft.

"He's from Toronto, all right, from the accounting section of the RCMP. The skinny blonde" (to men anything under a size 36 is skinny) "is from Detroit via Oslo and she's got a Soviet record a foot long." Mac detailed the rest and all but one were plants; the Commonwealth, South Africa, Belgium, and so on.

"What about the odd one?"

"One, just one. And this kid that looks twenty is actually thirty, has a record for shoplifting, narcotics, and prostitution in Plainsville, Ohio, and a face identical with the top graduate of Walsh Institute last year."

"Who was on his bucket?"

He didn't know—yet—but he'd find out. He admitted some of his own error when I prodded him. "All right, all right! So I thought it was a lot more important to get someone we can trust inside than to worry about the rest."

I began to laugh, and presently he saw the point. Two dozen phonies, all ready to spy on each other, and I was another. We parted on fairly good terms, and late that night when I checked the color around my hair roots I made up my mind to take up Jordan's offer of living quarters on Peche Island. Not even one single pass at me, hey?

## Chapter Eleven

Ken Jordan, blast his hide, was as good as his word. He used the direct method; he checked all the senior yearbooks of the high schools in the area, picked out all the prettiest girls and the sleekest young men, and offered them jobs at more than their parents were earning. He was smart enough to check their scholastic records, which I didn't know at the time when the first dewy-eyed kids showed up for whatever orientation I felt I should give them. When I protested to Jordan that these kids were barely dry behind the ears, he just laughed.

"The younger the better," he said. "No bad habits to unlearn, and lots of brains, I understand. Lots more than I had at that age."

"So," I asked him, "what does which and to whom?"

An airy wave. "Try them out around the loop until you find the right slot. If they don't work out on any job, come back to me and tell me 'I told you so,' sugar."

"Sugar?" I glared at him.

He stood up and bowed. "Like the fat boy is Skinny and the bald guy is Curly. There'll be a big tall beard here tomorrow from the University of Michigan with the results of a whole slew of aptitude tests."

I hadn't thought he'd have that much sense. "What's his name, or do I just call him Beard?"

"Wrote it down. Have it here someplace. . . . I'll call you this afternoon if I find it. Anyway, he's all cleared with the Burns guards. I'll see you, sugar," and he walked out, and a few minutes later I heard the eerie shriek of the hovercraft turbines off to Canada.

Basically, he might be a decent slob, but at that very minute I hated his guts. Ruining the carefully planted staff we had ready, he'd rejected the whole bunch to foist off on me a mob if immature high school kids to hire, to train, and to worry about. I leafed through some of the photos he had tossed on my desk. Why, some of these kids weren't old enough to have a paper route! Then I remembered that these were the cream of their schools, with no bad habits, at least in a business sense, to overcome. And when I got to the bottom of the pile I was madder yet; these girls were all absolute danger signals. Alongside any one of them I looked like a well-stored prune. Youth, when you're that close to thirty, is one enormous pain where you don't scratch in public. So, feeling every minute of my age, I made copies of the photos and data for the United States government to start checking on.

Jordan showed up a week later.

He'd hired the chief buyer from Marshall Fields, the chief buyer and his assistant from J. L. Hudson's, miscellaneous persons from Toronto, Vancouver, and a Peruvian named Almirante O'Higgins from the University of Lima. Those I had no ground to resent, as they were all at least my age, and several much older, and all male. Off he went again in his British jet (it was interesting to read in the papers how much fuss the Australians made over him, and how the mobs tried to touch his hand and tear his clothes in Hongkong) and came back with more personnel. Apparently he got tired of opening his own beer, which he now seemed to prefer to the fusel he'd been raised on, and his jet now had a stewardess trained by Air Cathay. When she first met me I took one stunned look at how the cheongsam showed everything up to her navel; when she was fitted with the shortie-kilts that all the Regan-employed females had to wear, she looked even better, which cheered me not at all.

And it was a good long time before someone, playing with a computer, noted that not one new Regan employee was married. Some of the older ones had been in the tub, true, but had been widowed or divorced. This fact caused a great deal of surmise, but I paid no attention to it, having once been married myself. Besides, I was busy.

Find immediate living quarters for most (the youngest ones were living at home with the parental agreement that they could move to the island when facilities were completed. Jordan *did* put up a small hall and told the kids he'd pay for the furniture and the layout if they'd pick out what they wanted, and they promptly went crazy. Did you ever walk into a room styled by an eighteen-year-old?). Build a restaurant, *not* a cafeteria. Build a three-story office building. Stock them both. (I might as well here admit that Jordan knew restaurant food better than I did; on the grounds that any food gets boring, he had great fun bringing cooks from all over the world for three-month periods, but that was after we got rolling.) Build a bowling alley, a heated swimming pool (with the polluted Detroit River at the front and back doors), and a dance hall—so help me, pocket size, but still a dance hall. Build four bars (four!), one at each corner of the office building, each in a different style. Buy sheets and pillowcases, knives and forks, pool cues and tennis nets. I crawled the walls at first, because every time I had a list complete Jordan came along with another brilliant thought which he considered essential. He thought everything he wanted was essential. But he could afford it.

I was only saved from the rubber room (even though Jordan once pulled the main power switch when he caught me working what he considered too late) by Jordan's own forethought. I poured the whole kettle into the collective laps of the buyers and planners who were loafing comfortably in their paid-for Statler suites; they were bored, and the competent commercial experts took over. They were lot tougher on the construction contractor and vendors than I had time to be. It even got to the point where one of the high schools kids (or two or three at times) would operate the PBX I'd had the telephone company install, switch the calls to the right place, and I would sit and wonder just what in hell this Ken Jordan was going to think up next.

He ambled in, wandered out, flitted his jet toy around the world, usually taking a couple of the cuter high schoolers just for the ride and many times different new employees to look at whatever they wanted. His first trip, there had been a fooforaw at landing with no passports, but at the next United Nations meeting the various member nations agreed to accept Regan passports instead of national passports from where the individuals had originated. But passports they wanted; Ken Jordan might not need one (with the sight of that fantastic landing ship in their memories), but they still wanted passports for the polloi. All right, Jordan must have said to himself, and he showed up with a sheaf of blank forms patterned after the standard U.S. passport. He tossed them to me to keep in my drawer—we didn't even have a safe! He laughed at me when I said we needed one—and of course I promptly lifted a handful for future purposes. Every solitary one was limp and cruddy when I turned them over to Mac an hour later.

Back to my drawer they went, and the next day they were again fresh and crisp. After a few more tries Mac turned a few over to the lab where the experts pounded their heads on the floor when, despite everything they could do including vacuum and low temperatures, the passports forms quietly and quickly rotted into dust. Mac told me later that he had been *ordered* to duplicate or find out the formula for this wonder document, and was only saved by the fact that we were now certain that Jordan was in contact with his Regan Group. No ship had landed, no terrestrial art was equal to his paper, so he had a contact. Who? Where?

The piledrivers finished thumping around the island's edge, the new buildings were completed and almost ready for occupancy, and the very last things the construction crews did before they cleaned up the clutter was to dig a hole close to the center of our territory. Some twenty feet deep, at my closest guess it was slightly longer in both dimensions; it rained the very same night, leaving the Burns guards reeking wet and the hole almost half full. Since the hole was well below the island waterline, I was vaguely surprised it was not brimful, but Ken Jordan had strolled over and was unimpressed. By this time I wouldn't have been shocked if he stocked it with coelecanths. Nor wondered why a bulldozer and Towmotor were left parked alongside the pit.

About noon the next day the squealing and howling of the high schoolers I had working around the place brought me out in the open. The space ship was landing.

It was just as impressive as the first time I had seen it, even more now that it was the real thing and not on a thirty-six-inch screen. It settled right alongside the hole, where Jordan and other men were waiting. The Burns guards, there in force, were panting, red in the face, as they deserted their watchmen's posts. The same "gangplank"—it had to be called that—swung down, carrying something I could not see from my angle as I hurried to the site, with the teenagers scampering and galloping ahead as we raced to see the show. There was little detail to see, as we found out; only a large roundish ball that hung on the gangplank edge defying gravity. It was grayish and metallic, with no openings or projections as far as I could make out, and I tried hard because I knew this would be of later interest.

Jordan made no move, and the rounded glob chose that moment to roll off the gangplank and fall with a mighty splash into its watery grave. That was all there was to it; the side of the ship swung up again, Jordan motioned to one of the men who whined the starter motor until the big Cat caught. It coughed diesel smoke until the driver was satisfied, when he tramped on it, spun on one of his tracks, dropped his blade into the fill dirt, and started gouging to refill the hole. Now, what the hell, I thought, did he put in there? It was certainly waterproof, probably shockproof, and didn't look like anything but a worn ten-ton balloon. The teenagers gawped, got in the way of the bulldozer as it mauled, and just as I was ready to get their cute little rumps back to work the gangplank flipped down again.

The same grayish metal, but there the similarity ended. It was, as well as a nonmechanic can describe it, a mongrel cross of reels of telephone cable with a painter's ladder designed by a strabismic millwright. It posed awkwardly on the gangplank edge for a long time while the big Towmotor jockeyed back and forth until Jordan was satisfied with the position. Then the driver ran his forks under as far as he could, the rest of the crew climbed on the weird affair to chain it firmly to the truck, and it was amusing to see the various efforts to get a better look at what might be revealed inside the ship. I knew half of all the construction crews were federal men getting their hands dirty, and possibly all the rest was composed of other foreign nationals, which possibly explained the fact that all this past construction had been completed without one man-hour lost to labor trouble.

Everyone followed the truck as it waddled to the water's edge and waded in, the crew getting wet and Jordan along with them soaked to his waist. There was some thoughtful discussion, which I had heard before, but which caused awe among the high schoolers at hearing the words bellowed unashamedly in public. Then the Towmotor forks inched down the column until most of the contraption was under the water and my memory noted that here was the underwater foundation Jordan's piledrivers had built nine inches below low-water line, which at the present Detroit river level was about two feet higher. We watched eagerly while the men and Jordan himself took turns ducking their heads under, apparently trying to line up something with something else until the kids started tossing gravel and splashing water. With nothing to see but a static Towmotor in polluted water, I snarled at the youngsters until, with many curious looks over our shoulders, we started back to work. There were boats arriving offshore to see at first hand the spaceship that was still squatting by the snorting bulldozer, and the Burns guards had flocked belatedly back to the island watchposts. Far down the island I could see guards chasing people who had seized the chance to land and snoop. When I got into the office one of the kids swooped on me, one of the two operators breaking in on the PBX.

"Dana Iverson," she said, "come and look at this!" She tugged me into the PBX room.

The other girl sat there filled with awe. The buzzer was shrilling steadily and every single light on the board was lit: all incoming calls which the stunned girl was making no effort to answer. It was laughable. I walked over to switch off the audible signal unit, but the lights still glowed; some flickered and went out as the caller gave up, but immediately lit again with another call.

The girl at the board was ashen, and I patted her on the shoulder. "No problem. Take the calls one by one, don't get excited, tell the caller Ken Jordan and myself are unavailable, and hang up politely. If you can hang up politely, show me later how you did it."

That set the girls laughing. I looked again out in front to see the bulldozer still scraping, Jordan and his crew still splashing, and went in to call the Ontario provincials to see what they could do about keeping the goggling pleasure boats out of our waters. I wished the Regan Group had a navy.

Some time later when the teenagers had everything under control I walked back down to where Jordan and his crew were now standing, wearing contented smiles and soppy clothes. Almost in step with me rattled the bulldozer, the fill completed and the ship now standing alone. As I came up, Jordan said, "That should do it," and ducked his head under the water.

The gadget had been fastened in some fashion to the underwater foundations, and several feet of the cross-rodded structure bulked upward. The water was too roiled to see beneath the surface as Jordan's head popped up for air alongside the cable-like reels. Under again he went, to come up and wade to where I was standing.

"Got it," he announced. "Everybody through for the day." There was a flurry of activity and it took only a few minutes for the men to roll on the waiting barge the crawler, the Towmotor, the remaining tools, and for the barge to wind up its loading ramp. As the barge started to move away Jordan called, and waded over to hand up to the nearest crewman a wad of money. "The first half-barrel's on me," he said, and splashed back on shore. Naturally, everyone whooped, and the barge chugged away with good feelings on both sides. All the crews had seemed to like Jordan; he had always strolled around taking a mechanic's interest in operations, never afraid to pitch in and get grease on his silver pants. We all waved goodbye, and I noted several police boats patrolling the channel between our island and the Canadian shore. The water was poppyseeded with sightseers and in American waters loafed a Coast Guard cruiser and a harbor-master's speedboat of the Detroit police ran up and down the shallows with USCG helicopters overhead.

"You're soaked," I said.

"Yeah." He was eyeing the gadget thoughtfully.

I asked, "Is that thing just balanced on something?"

"It better not be; there's a slot like a Woodruff key—you don't know what that is?—just say a slot, and the merry-go-round fits in."

I thought I hadn't heard right. "Did you say merry-go-round?"

"That's what I call it. I know what it is, but I've never seen one."

Through Captain Lukkari's eyes or memory, I thought. "What is it? What's it supposed to do?"

He started to reply, but the gadget grunted, shuddered, and began to move. The water stirred in aimless circles at its base, and the whole dingus began to inch away, moving along the island rim, like an old man anxious not to get his pants cuffs muddy. I caught Jordan's expression at that instant; eager, expectant, and actually relieved.

I asked him again when the machine was a short distance away, still moving at the same stately pace like a asthmatic giraffe. "What's it supposed to do, anyway?"

"Nothing, right now," he said. "The first trip around it checks and clears the slot it's riding in. The second trip it goes to work."

"What kind of work?"

"You'll find out," and I think he was not teasing, almost not certain of what was on schedule. He shivered once in the river breeze and I suggested he go dry out and change clothes. He agreed, and with a last look at the machine, still gliding away steadily, we started back to our office building where the kids, when they saw us coming, beat us inside.

We had walked a hundred feet when he said abruptly, "Iverson, you do a pretty good job."

Equally shortly I said, "Thanks. What you hired me for."

He went on, "You've got a lifetime job if you want it."

"Thanks again. Until I get old and gray?"

"If you want it. Remember that. You in your new place yet?"

I pointed down the island. "You can't see it from

here. Behind that clump of palms. Why did you import those palm trees, anyway? You know they can't stand the cold."

He didn't answer, until we were at the office entrance. "Get everyone off the island tonight."

"What?" I said unbelievingly.

"The Burns guards, everyone. No one reports tomorrow."

"If you say so; everyone off, no work tomorrow. Cancel the Burns men's night shift tonight."

He shook his head. "Keep the night shift; put them in speedboats and have them cruise around the shoreline. Lights and flares and blank cartridges. No one gets within any distance of the island. Ask the Ontario police and the Coast Guard if they'll help."

"They're out there already."

"Good. This is important. Anyone close to the shoreline is apt to get hurt."

I didn't ask in what way. "Right. I'll keep both the hovercrafts working all night. They're a lot faster than anything else around. When do you want me to come back to work? I could maybe run up to Oscoda to see my relatives," of which I had none, but I knew Mac would want a long conference.

"Not you," he said. "I want you here."

"All right, Ken Jordan. Any particular reason, anything you want information on?"

"Maybe," was all he said. "I'm not sure."

"It's almost three o'clock. I'll have to move fast to set up the night patrol and kill everything for tomorrow," and I started into the office.

"Hold it. What time do you eat dinner?"

"Whenever I feel hungry. Frozen foods are fast, steak in the broiler if I'm hungry, cheese and crackers if I'm lazy. Are you asking me for information, or for a date? There are formal ways, you know." I felt a bit giddy, which was asinine.

He smiled faintly. "Not exactly. I thought you might like company, say around eight?" It was a question.

Then, dammit, it *was* a date. I played it soft. "Why not? Eight o'clock behind the palms. If I knew what a hibiscus was I'd have one behind my ear."

"We'll be there at eight."

Halfway through the door I swung back. "You said 'we'?"

He nodded, and my 'date' went up the flue. "Someone you should meet," and my glance flicked to the ship still motionless not far away. "Right," he said, "Lee Lukkari. Any objections?"

"No," I said quickly. "No objections," and I walked inside.

## Chapter Twelve

Almost exactly at eight there was a tap on my door. I took a fast look around (after all, everything was so new I wasn't certain what should be where), and opened the door for Captain Lee Lukkari . . . alone.

She said, "You are Dana Iverson."

"And you're Captain Lee Kay Lukkari. Please come in."

She stepped gracefully inside and I left the door open in case Jordan was on his way.

Her voice was lilting, pleasant, with the accent I had heard on TV. "I feel that I know you well, Dana Iverson; myself and Ken have had some discussion about you."

"Discussion?"

"Perhaps the wrong word? But we have talked about you."

"It would have been nice to eavesdrop. Sit down, won't you, Captain?"

"Thank you," and her glance darted around. "Where would you like me to sit?"

"There, if you like," pointing to my new favorite chair that Jordan had paid far too much for, and she slid into the chair with a liquid motion. Being female myself most of the time, I took plenty of time to offer her drinks and give her a much more searching examination than the TV image had allowed. She shaded five six a fraction without the sloped sandals, the silver hair was either kosher or she had a beauty shop on her cruiser, the way her breasts jiggled when she moved showed them natural, her legs were firm and her knees unblemished, a slim waist and a proportioned rump meshed, under her kilt high on her right thigh was a flat case—*Life* had been accurate—and the silver panties that matched the rest of her uniform showed she didn't wear, didn't need a girdle. I hated her.

She thanked me for the beer. For her, it tasted just as good as it would to Ken Jordan. She, surprisingly, took one of my cigarettes and sat back. I knew I had been cataloguing her too openly for tact and probably for her taste. Lightly she opened the conversation. "Are you sure you wouldn't like to check if you are recording properly?"

This shocker sent my glance, just like the man who denied he stole the watch, promptly to the bedroom where the tape recorder was stashed. I took a big gulp of beer while I sought the right thing to say.

"I guess you have me cold," I admitted. "You must be a mind-reader."

And to my horror she said, "Sometimes."

Was she bluffing? Was her glance as honest as they come? Mind-reading!

She produced a charming stage grimace. "Who do you really work for, Dana Iverson? The government of what used to be Ken's group—the United States government? Yes, I see you do."

I managed to get out, "Captain Lukkari—"

"No, Lee Lukkari. *Kay* means I am captain, in our language. Ken misunderstood me when we first met.

Lee Lukkari is my name; *Kay*, a title which I have been given. You must be an important person in your group; how long have you been working as a spy? Five years, ten? I see; five, or a little more."

She was quite fluent, splitting words like mis-un-der-stood and im-por-tant in a breathy way. But I caught every fatal word.

Oh, hell. "So I'm dead. What happens now?"

A startled glance. "Dead?" Then she relaxed. "You used a word in a diff-er-ent way. No, you are not 'dead,' Dana Iverson. Or maybe you have been 'dead' a longer time than you imagine." Incredibly, she swigged down her beer and I, the perfect hostess, got up to open another bottle.

"You are surprised, Dana Iverson? This is natural. It was also in-ev-it-a-ble for the government of your group, or any group, with Earth men-tal-ity, to try to insert a spy. You enjoy be-ing a spy?"

Well, hang for a sheep. "It's a living."

She blew smoke at the ventilator. "Yes, I sup-pose it is one meth-od. . . . You realize why I came alone?"

"No," I said honestly, "I don't. You're going to tell Ken Jordan, regardless."

She shook her head, and silver curls flashed. "No need. Ken has known since one fraction after you first met. But we did not expect a spy so soon, nor one so deliciously feminine. Your organization is extremely efficient."

"About half as efficient," I said sourly, "as I thought it was. I like the 'deliciously feminine,' but what do you mean, 'a fraction after we first met'? That's physically impossible."

"Exactly. Physically impossible." She stood up easily, flipped up her skirt to her waist (her crotch was either hairless or shaved, with no dark patch), did something to the little kit I had glimpsed on her thigh, handed me a tiny piece of a jigsaw puzzle, and sat down again, lazily comfortable with her legs tucked under her, the way I sit when I'm reading. She said "I'm ninety years old, I can read your mind, and I am going to hurt you before I leave. These are lies, but now I am telling the truth."

Only, by Judas, I knew it before she told me.

I looked down at the wafer I was holding. I didn't know by its weight or its feel if it were metal or plastic. But I know that when she was talking I knew whether or not she was lying. I *knew* it.

"This should come in very handy," I said grimly. "You make me out very stupid. Also my bosses," an afterthought.

Lee Lukkari tilted her head. "You were told our Regan Group needs no weapons. And we have none. But we do have tools."

The thing in my hand told me she was truthful. Hold it! How did I know the gadget was not rigged for that exact purpose? I mentioned that.

She spread her palms in an Oriental gesture. "That is a tool. Tampering—and that is impossible even to Regan tech-nol-o-gy—would impair the function of the tool."

She swigged thirstily. Jordan had taught her some earthy habits. I said tentatively, the shock of exposure still numbing me, "Why did you show me this? Aren't you afraid I'll run off with it? Anyone would give her soul for this."

"Would she? In our Regan Group millions died in one revolution and two wars, almost a whole generation went inwardly mad when faced with reality, before this—lie detector, you would call it—was completely accepted. This only on my own planet. Other peoples in our Regan Group reacted the same, no matter at what stage in their history. Do you want it?"

I thought about it briefly and then shuddered. "Not right now," and handed it back.

She refused it. "Keep it, and you know I do not lie. Besides," as she smiled pleasantly, "its power will be exhausted shortly. This precaution I did take," and her grin was satanic.

I turned the wafer over in my fingers. "You weren't sure. So you don't know everything."

She leaned over and looked into my eyes. "We know very little. We know only what we see, what we are told, most of which is a fiction." Suddenly she stood up and did things to her blouse. "We must talk, Dana Iverson. You will drink and talk with me and we will be comfortable. Your god can damn this brah-seer. It is for ornament. Ken says most women wear binders around their ass—this is not a right word from your face?"

I began to laugh. "Not out in public. A man has an ass, or he can be one and usually is; but theoretically a woman has a—the ads call it a derrière. From these kids he hired, I thought Ken Jordan was a tit man."

She cocked her head at my comedy. "This is a joke. I will find out what is fun-ny. We will talk?" She sat back luxuriously, happily scratched under each perfect breast, and kicked her shoes off. "You will ask me what you want to know. Either as female to female or as Earth to Regan. You will know I am telling the truth."

And the first thing that came to my mind was, "You don't usually wear many clothes, do you?"

"Very little. My home is warm, much warmer than here. It is even now cool for me, only I must get these

Earth clothes removed because I sweat and I itch, es-pecially this goddam brah-seer."

"We call it a bra."

"Goddam bra. You wear one."

"Our standards. How can you get along—"

She waved me away. "Of course, not always. When we work, or are active, we must not . . . flop, is the word? But, every day, to tie myself in? Because of your customs, Ken was very surprised when he first saw me in my ship."

I could just see him waking to see her figure in the middle of a Jordan hangover. "I'll bet he was. Why do you wear Earth clothes, then?"

"Your tel-e-vision programs, partly; your stress on female bodies, or sections. And mostly from Ken, of course, who remembered how short the skirts were, and how much he enjoyed looking under them when he was much younger. We, like you, know much about stage management."

I quoted the recent magazines. "And skirts are shortening up again, ever since you landed. Including every fat woman who looks terrible."

She was unimpressed. "I am not fat, and neither are you."

I said, "Is all the Regan Group like you?"

"On my planet, yes. Others, yes and no."

"What are *they* like?"

She said instantly, "I will not tell."

I tried once more. "How about the men, the males on your own planet?"

She giggled. "Very nice," but then she sobered. "Very nice," she repeated.

I caught the inflection. "And one, especially."

Lee Lukkari changed positions easily, like a kitten. "No. No one. I have been training for my captaincy for some years."

"Years?"

"Many years." She looked at the smoke curling from her cigarette and stubbed it out. "This you should know. It is an honor to me, to my family, to my own group within our Regan Group to be chosen to be trained for my job. Because of what you hold in your hand, our lie detector, it is an award—many apply, some are accepted for further training, a few fulfill their possibilities. I say possibilities, because we have never been able, despite the best efforts of our experts, to test someone and say *there* is the slot you should occupy; latent ability may be there, but the promise may not be fulfilled. Let me say I worked hard, and I was lucky. May I have more of your beer? Thank you.

"You asked me about the men of my planet. I tell you I have never formed a permanent attachment with any male. No, that was a choice, it was not my program but my desire. You will understand, Dana Iverson?"

Sure, I understood. Once I'd had the same choice but I'd made the wrong one. But there was still something wrong about this whole Lukkari situation; what was it? When my cigarette ashes fell in my lap I realized she hadn't said anything recently. I looked up and she was staring.

I said, "Something bothers me, Lee Lukkari; this tells me only you are telling the truth; it does not tell me what's really on your mind."

"That is true. You have questions?"

"Certainly I have questions. One, in particular, bothers me. You knew all along I was not what I claimed. Why did you expose me now? Or why did you expose me at all? Why not feed me just what you want me to know, while I think I'm getting everything? The standard technique, which I'm sure you use."

She nodded quickly. "You are efficient and you are clever. You are also essential to our Regan Group. You, or someone very like you, is a solution to a standard problem that I dreaded to have much more difficulty in even approaching. You understand what I am saying? I—Ken or I—am offering you a job worthy of your skills and a reward far beyond what you expected."

"Oh, come on, now," I said, although I knew she was not lying. "What's this great big juicy reward?"

"You haven't guessed? Regan citizenship, and quite probably your life."

"What do you mean, my life?"

"Just that. Stay alive far past the time you would die naturally, stay alive with full physical and mental capabilities until your body wears out completely. Of course, then you will be willing to die."

"And how old is that?"

"I will not tell—yet."

"And if I don't?"

She sighed. "I am not sure. But all my training, all my knowledge, tells me you die by violence very shortly."

"That's a hell of a thing to tell anybody. How do you know?"

"I do not *know*. But I am *sure*."

This time I wanted more beer, lots of it, and I sneaked in a shot on the side. "Let me get this straight. You're offering me a job. Doing what?"

"I will surprise you," she said. "Doing exactly what you are doing now, with a little different attitude."

"My attitude I was born with," I snapped angrily. "I've done a job, I get paid, my attitude and what I do off the job is my own business." I challenged her.

"Ken Jordan today told me I did a good job. What's 'attitude' got to do with it?"

She stood up and shivered lightly. "I am chilled," and she twirled the silver blouse carelessly around her before she curled up again in the big chair. "I change the subject for a moment. You will shortly see why.

"You know I have all Ken's memories in me, and he has mine? Your eyes, close them for a fraction and dream. You are young. You are normal. You want love, your body *needs* love, you want children, a home. Suddenly you know your male, not partially, but completely. All your life you have been trained for this male, long even before you know who he might be. But now your time is here, and you know him; every desire, his want, his hopes, his every experience. Because you are so interested and so eager you explore his memory and find things even he has forgotten he knew. You can image that?

"That is not all. This male now knows you the same way. He knows what makes you smile, what makes you happy, where and how a touch of his finger or a laugh or a twist of his body can paralyze you with joy. You can imagine that, Dana Iverson?

"Then imagine, if you can, ever trying to exist without that male!"

I opened my eyes which I had sportingly closed. "I certainly can image that. I felt like that myself ten years or so ago. But there's another side, Lee Lukkari, which you haven't found out. *You* imagine this male, knowing everything you hate, that makes you unhappy, that rips you up and down, that makes you sick with fear and makes you scream. Imagine this male liking to hurt you, liking not the things you like but wanting to hurt, wanting to inflict pain."

Her face was somber, her voice low. "Yes, I imagine

that. I close my eyes and visualize these events, anticipate pain. . . . But this is my education. It is my price I can, I want to pay for my Regan Group. It is a tiny possibility, but such things have happened, and they could happen again."

I said, "So what has all this got to do with me?"

The flat palms. "You are being deliberately obtuse. I have been describing myself and Ken Jordan."

"That drunk?"

For an instant she wore the expression I used to use when my ex-husband started crawling up the back stairs. "You have noticed a reduction in Ken's drinking?"

As a matter of fact, I had. He had four well-stocked bars in arm's reach, but lately he had stuck to Dortmunder beer.

"He gets headaches when he drinks your whiskey, as I do without chemical precautions, as I used in your United Nations Group party. Your beer (which I call *tek*) is much like ours with a much more happy flavor. So we can drink together now."

"Don't you ever get the idea he can't get schnockered on beer."

"So can I. Sometimes it is pleasant to get—what?"

"Schnockered. Drunk. My father used to use that word."

"I will remember. But this is the first indication, and I am glad. There will be other indications, then more, and then he will be more like me and I like him. Then each will be no longer a half, but together a whole."

I shook my head. "You make this soak sound like Little Boy Blue."

"I know of Little Boy Blue. It is one of Ken's memories so old he has forgotten. He will never be a little boy again. But he still has a little boy in him, like every man."

Which irritated me all to hell. To hear someone like Lee Lukkari talk this way about some Skid Row bubblehead was sheer idiocy, and if all women of the Regan Group were like her, we'd made a bad mistake all around. I got up to close the front door I'd left open for Jordan. It was getting chilly.

"I want to get something straight. From what you say, I get the impression that you want, that you need Ken Jordan. I'm not flattering you and you know it, but why would anyone like you want a wornout old alcoholic—all right, a reforming alcoholic—within ten feet of her? It's all in your head, certainly not in that ancient carcass of his! And if you want that soak around you, why don't you just pick him up and fly off the edge around the moon or somewhere? And what have I got to do with it?"

I still had the wafer in my hand when she said, "Last things first. Your file says you are twenty-eight years old, Dana Iverson."

"Twenty-nine," I said grudgingly, "which I'm going to be all the rest of my life."

"These years," she counted, "are each equal to one turn of your planet around your sun. I am younger than you. By my numbers I am twenty-six—"

"You see what I mean? Ken Jordan was born forty-two years ago, and looks fifty in a dim light."

She was unperturbed. "Twenty-six years. But my sun is bigger and much warmer, and my planet turns around my sun in two point two one of your years."

That, more than anything she had said or done up until then, did more to bring home to me how completely alien she was, not just a half-naked sexy blonde in a dancer's skirts. Almost sixty years old! I suspected the wafer I was holding, but down deep I knew better. The body, the face, the skin, that careless attitude of youth—I would have said she was my own age if I felt feline, but all along I would have told myself she was in her early twenties.

I carried it off fairly well. "That makes you fifty-seven years and a bit." I tried to disguise the surprise, the envy in my voice, but I couldn't. "Doesn't that make you sort of a baby-snatcher?"

She leaned back and began to laugh as hard as she could. Even with her mouth open she still looked as lovely as a pixie. "A baby-snatcher? Fifteen of your years, less than half of that of ours?" She went off again, and damn her, she sounded like Peter Pan's music box trilling away. At last she said, "You pardon me, Dana Iverson. At home a difference in age much greater is nothing," and she leaned toward me for emphasis. "You are not observant—perhaps you have been too busy? You have not noticed that Ken seems younger, healthier, easier to deal with. You have not seen the inside of his body where flaws have been corrected. You have not seen dangerous animals (you call them germs) removed, the beneficial ones increased. You have not seen, because you are too close, the changes that have started. Do I know what you are going to say? No, he will not grow younger. His outside appearance will not change—not until a great deal longer than he would have lived if my cruiser KAYTA had not landed. Several of his organs, I do not know your names, were on the very verge and had to be rebuilt."

"All right," I said thickly. "So you're Superwoman. You've got your own private Superman hatching. You know who I am, you know what I was doing, you'll still be young and beautiful while I'm rotting underground. You've made your point so many times I'm nauseated. Now, will you take that young little ass out that door before I cram a beer bottle down your throat?" When I finished I was screaming.

I was so furious I only heard the door open. When I looked up to glare, she was standing with one hand on the doorknob, the other dangling the discarded bra, and she looked sorry when she said, "Please don't try to leave tonight—it would be very dangerous."

"Get out," I said tightly, and my voice started up the scale. "Get out. Get out! Get *out*!" And she was gone before the bottle crashed against the door.

## Chapter Thirteen

When I got up in the morning I had the grandmother of all headaches. I got up to wash down four aspirins with pineapple juice, and went back to bed to let the aspirin take effect. It was light outside, and the birds were squeaking as they do in the early dawn. I knew I would be in severe trouble by losing my Regan Group position, almost immediately thereafter losing my importance to my government, and Mac, my federal boss, would be getting transferred to Rock Island or Lower Mousetrap. Things chased themselves around in my head until I managed to drift back to restless sleep.

I got up permanently when the clock said ten. It was noon by the time I'd showered and packed, and there wasn't enough room in my bags for my clothes, let alone one tenth of the things I'd picked up over the last few years. I'd have to leave them and make some arrangements to have them shipped later. Shipped to where? I didn't know and didn't care, and probably the best thing for me to do would be to get another job; not with the government, because my name there would be as dirty a word as Mac's. Well, to hell with it. I had saved almost all my Regan salary and if I quit the federal government I'd have my pension savings that I could draw out. I remembered I had left several things in my office desk; some Regan data that Mac might want to see and a fancy clock-barometer I'd picked up in Zurich. That I wanted, and I walked out to pick up at the office what I wanted. When I shut the door behind me I realized that I'd automatically worn the Regan kilts, but with my regular clothes now packed I had no intention of stripping and re-dressing and repacking. Jordan could afford, anyway, to lose a skirt and blouse.

Halfway through the five-minute walk the stillness made an impression on me. Normally, the Detroit River is a busy place with small boats squawking their horns, big ore freighters using their steam whistles, and an occasional traffic murmur from Windsor's Riverside Drive a few hundred yards away. I stopped, cocking an ear to listen. The birds were chirping, the trees rustling, but there seemed to be something muffling the normal background noises. I couldn't account for it, and after pausing a few seconds I went on. I came out into the open, noted that the spaceship was still spotted in the same place and that offshore there were more small boats than there had ever been. Some of them were quite close, trying to see what was going on, trying to get close because there was a slight mist on the water. Come up close, I thought sardonically, I might need a ride home, and I went into the office to collect my things. It didn't take long to clean out my desk, take a last look around—not a sad look, just habit—and try to raise someone on the telephones. The lines were dead. Oh, swell, I thought. Now I tell Jordan I quit, but please row me back to shore. Well, he could do that much. I walked out, shut the door behind me, and started back to my house. It was quiet outside, but my mind ignored that, and the box of junk I was carrying was not heavy but awkward.

Then something inside me said urgently, "Behind you!" and I spun. There was an ugly black shadow diving directly at me. I panicked.

The box went one way, I went another, rolling off the path into thick grass, knowing I was many feet from overhead cover, hoping the black thing would miss me on a second pass, scrabbling frantically at the grass for a foothold, and then as my right toe-tip skidded on the damp grass I fell flat on my back, belly up, completely helpless.

The shadow did not come back. It couldn't, because it was only a shadow. Far up, at an angle to me, was the ungainly machine that Jordan had set up the previous day. It was suspended in air, at least a hundred feet high, scooting along the island edge. In midair? As I laid there on my back I took another look around. The mist I had noticed before was not a mist. It was a wall.

Sheepishly, but with my heart still pounding furiously from the adrenalin in my veins, I got up and tried to brush myself off. My knees were green from where I had fallen, my skirt was grass-stained, and two fasteners were ripped from my blouse. I looked around and saw no one, stuffed the bottom of my blouse back where it belonged, and walked down to the water's edge. I slipped off the Regan shoes, ripped off my nylons, which were beyond repair, and waded out to touch the transparent mist. It was solid.

I ran my hands over it. I looked through it. It was solid, smooth, and almost completely transparent. I tried to scratch it, using a sharp stone I picked up, and made no impression or mark. I banged it with a bigger rock; nothing. I looked up. It was tall as a good-sized building, curving inward slightly. Around the west end of the island, far up in the air, I saw the machine coming again. It looked like an octopus or a bat clinging to a wall, tentacles hanging down, menacing. Hurriedly I backed away, belatedly remembering that Jordan had warned me about danger. Then I remembered the binoculars I had dropped with my box I had taken from my old office, the ones I'd bought when I'd first moved onto the island and had spent hours watching the passing ships. I raced back to where I had tripped, gathered up my things to stack them back in the carton, found the binoculars, and went back, not too close, to the shoreline. I found a good spot where I could brace my elbows, focused as close as I could because the upper edge of the wall was all but invisible, and waited for the monster to make another pass. In a few minutes it came into view again.

The parts that looked like ladders had unfolded stretching up and out from the core of the machine. Hanging down were tubes or cables unreeled from the cylinders, trailing and dragging behind in the river water. The machine was riding on the top edge of the wall, the arms extended up and back. I focused as close as I could on a moving object and caught the sun's reflections until it became clear that the arms were exuding more of the wall itself. As it neared me, perfectly soundless, the same shadow preceded it and flickered away, the same shadow caused by the sun that had frightened me so much. It came directly down the beach line, over my head, and not till it passed did I realize that, with the wall curving inward, if that thing ever lost its balance I'd be crushed. By then it was gone.

I stayed there quite some time, going back once to my house to dig out my Bolex with the telephoto lens to get as much of it as I could. It was moving as fast as the average man would jog, each trip squirting out probably ten vertical feet or so of new wall. I tried to time several circuits, each time getting a different answer, and on some circuits it was gone so long I was almost certain it had fallen off or quit for the day. I sat there a good part of the afternoon, watching and using every roll of movie film I had. When I developed a crick, I gave up watching, stood up to stretch and to gather my camera and binoculars and other things, and walked stiffly back to my house. I'd have to see Jordan, I knew, to leave the island. If not right away, as soon as I could. He was probably frolicking in the silent spaceship with his Captain Lee Lukkari, I thought, and who was having the most fun taking care of who? But he wasn't.

He—and Lee Lukkari—were lying on their bellies on the grass in front of my house, playing some sort of game that involved shifting little stones from one pile to another. They were so giggly-intent that I watched them silently for several minutes before they noticed me. Jordan looked up, grinned, swept the stones together with a careless gesture, rolled over, and stood up.

"Hi," he said. "Been waiting for you," and he extended a hand down to his captain, who used it to pull herself up and began to brush off her skirt. I said nothing while I watched her lean over to brush Jordan off. Maternally?

He said, "I hear you quit."

I said, "That's right."

He brought out cigarettes, handed the package to Lee Lukkari, and he held a lighter for both of them. "No rule against it, sugar. But you can't leave right now. How about bringing a couple of chairs out in the sun and we'll talk it over?"

"If you want," I said, and went after some folding chairs. When we all sat down, me in the shade of the house and them in the sunlight, I said, "I still quit."

He shrugged. "I won't ask why. But you're cutting your own throat."

"Perhaps. But it's my own throat. I still quit."

Jordan looked steadily at me. "That was no figure of speech. Cutting your own throat, death by violence . . . I mean it."

"Oh, for God's sake!" I exploded. "Don't be such a stuffed shirt! So you're a thousand years ahead of me. Don't tell me you can read the future with a little glass ball. Don't tell me—"

"Shut up. Nobody said I could read the future. But I can add two and two. No reason why you can't use your head." He wouldn't let me get a word in. "You're an agent of the United States government, the only inside man in our Group. You're the only one that was in here while we put the wall up—"

"Wall?"

"You were down on the beach watching the wall go up. Shut up. You go back to your boss and tell him you quit. You've cut off his only source of information, of your own free will. You have lost your only value to your boss and his boss, again of your own free will. Why? Have you been brainwashed, if you want to use an old word, or has something been done to you without your knowing it? How long do you think you'd spend with the psychiatrists and the doctors proving you were or weren't? What's in your mind that they can try to get out?"

He was right, of course. I'd seen research teams at work on agents who had been treated by the Opposition and later escaped—or had been released. By the time they had been "examined" by the medics for information (or booby traps), they weren't much good anymore as agents or people.

And he kept hammering, his voice soft and easy, piling fact on fact while Captain Lukkari watched and said nothing. "Finally, after everything inside your head has been laid bare as deep as they can go, you'll be turned loose. Turned loose as a second-class citizen, someone who let her group down just when she was most needed, someone just one step short of a rat, and someone that may be technically free but who will still be watched every minute in case there might be something that was missed the first time around."

This, I knew, was standard practice, but I hadn't quite got around to realizing it might one day apply to myself.

"Yes, you'll be watched—but not well enough. Some other group will eventually snatch you up, take you to where *their* doctors and psychiatrists can work you over, hoping they'll discover something the first inquisition missed. Maybe you live through it, maybe you don't. Who cares? It's better if you don't, because if you're turned loose as being of no value you're headed for the same thing again with your own group to see what the second group may have found."

I hate women who cry, and to my disgust I felt tears forming, I felt so sorry for myself. I got up and walked into the house and sat in the bathroom for some time. When I came back out both of them were still sitting patiently.

I said, "You seem to have my future all planned out."

He didn't smile. "Yes. Things do happen, Dana Iverson, just like that. This is almost a certainty. Do you want your life, your personality, to be extinguished uselessly?"

I found the words hard to say, as I had always hated to be weak. "No, I don't. But I can't stay here, knowing you spotted me, without relaying that to my supervisor."

"Naturally," he agreed. "Your group would want to know every turn of events; they would accept your information, file it away (wondering why I still employed you), and at the very first opportunity they'd subject you to exactly the same treatment as they would if you walked in and informed them you resigned voluntarily."

I smoothed my hand nervously over my skirt, the short Regan kilt. I could feel every crease, every thread of the material. Jordan was sitting expectantly on the light lawn chair, Captain Lukkari's face was as unmoving as that of a beautiful Dresden doll. I took a deep breath. "What do you want–" Jordan quickly shook his head. "What do you suggest?"

Jordan leaned back and relaxed in the chair; the captain's face seemed to be softer. "How about a beer, sugar?"

Obediently I brought out beer and an opener, making myself an extrastiff drink in my kitchen. I felt as low as I'd ever felt in my life. I felt licked, worn out, beaten. I felt like a servant. I knew I was going to cry and wondered how long I could hold off the tears.

He drank off the bottle at a gulp. He said, "What do I suggest? That you quit–quit the United States government and become a true Regan Group employee."

I said, "I don't understand."

Jordan grinned. "It's not too hard. . . ." He leaned forward. "I have to have someone I can trust, not just the hired hand who carries the stock to the machine. I've got to have someone who acts Earth and thinks Regan, some one who's smart and capable, who can look at the good and bad and pick out the best for Regan, who can do the sort of capable work you've done so far, someone who can't be bribed, someone—me, in other words, when I'm not here." He finished the bottle and opened another.

"There's lots of things, Dana Iverson, that are going to happen; lots of things that must remain a secret among Regans. I need someone like you to work for me, to trust, to rely on. I need your capabilities, but I must have your loyalty ahead of anything else. Ahead of your government, ahead of your planet. Your thinking must be for Regan. It's as plain as that."

I said, "I've done a good job for you, I thought."

"Sure," he said. "Thanks to you, I'm far ahead of schedule. But reports smuggled to those that could very well become enemies—no, not included in the deal. You go Earth, or you go Regan."

"In other words," I said slowly, "you want me to be what my boss would call a traitor."

"Oh, hell," he snorted. "Some of your ancestors came from Ireland, some came from Germany. Were they traitors because they went to a better place to live? I don't want information from you, I want you to think and work Regan."

"In what way?"

"How in hell would I know?" he said impatiently. "But things might—will—happen where Regan thinking is important, essential. You're going to keep on running the joint, you know. What did you think I wanted you for?"

I hadn't known I was that important, and said so.

He brushed that away. "Everybody's important. I need you and I need your loyalty to Regan, now and in the future." He speared a glance at me. "What's in it for you? Regan citizenship. That includes medical treatments. It includes Regan protection, it includes

Regan knowledge, as much of it as you want or you need. And it includes transportation to wherever in our Regan Group you want to go, and a Regan pension, if you want to call it that, when you want to retire—if you want to retire."

Abruptly he stood up, leaving half his beer in the bottle alongside his chair. "Simplify it. Emigrate—at least mentally—to our Regan Group. Trade your present as a spy for a future as a Regan woman. Trade death or sickness for a long life, much longer; trade premature old age for a long pleasant career. Trade the tin dime for a gold dollar. You still can't leave the island until tomorrow, probably. You have that long to think it over. Coming?" He said to Captain Lukkari, and he walked briskly away.

The Captain, who had never taken her eyes from me, stood up. She said, quite clearly, "I'm sure you already know what your decision should be," and she went around the corner of the house after Jordan.

I carried the debris and the chairs back into the house. I walked down to the beach after a while and watched the sand and the water and the milling boats and counted the times the machine passed over my head. When it got dark I went back to the house and sat in the kitchen with the lights out, watching the big red neon ball on top of the Penobscot Building in downtown Detroit. I don't know what time it was when I unpacked all my things, hung them up or put them in drawers, and went to bed.

## Chapter Fourteen

I was almost through with my toast and coffee the next morning when Jordan tapped on my open door. I asked him in and poured him a cup of coffee.

"Toast, too," he said, and I dropped two slices of bread into the toaster. He looked around the kitchen, at me, and I was obscurely pleased I'd put makeup on before breakfast, which ordinarily I never do. "I guess you've made up your mind to stay."

I said I had, and the toast popped up for buttering.

"Questions I have to ask," apologetically. "You want to become a Regan citizen? No, you don't have to answer."

"The lie detector?"

"Sure thing. Inside me someplace; handier, don't have to carry it around ... You intend to become a Regan citizen, but you are not sure you want to; you're undecided. If you become a Regan citizen, will you take on the responsibilities that go with it? Have you any thought about backing out or becoming a Regan citizen for any reason like spying or obtaining information? Do you intend to wholeheartedly work for my Regan Group to the best of your ability?"

There were many other questions along the same

line. None of them required more than a simple yes or no, and usually he knew my answer before I could open my mouth. At first I felt uncomfortable, as though he was really reading my mind, but then I felt easier as he finished his rapid-fire questions. As he pushed his coffee cup across for a refill he said easily and casually, "Are you very much afraid of dying? Are you afraid of pain?"

I almost dropped the coffeepot.

He said, "I thought you took that little lecture yesterday a lot too seriously and too quickly. Do you want to tell me why you're not particularly afraid of death, but the thought of pain almost makes you black out? This is none of my business, kid, and it hasn't anything to do with the Regans. But it might be better if I knew why. Think you can tell me?"

It all flooded back at me. "My ex-husband. He was not only a drunk, he was a sadist." I stood up, hoisted my skirt, pulling down my panties as I half turned.

He gave one quick look at my left cheek. "Initials. 'W.I.' "

I let the panties flip back up and smoothed down the skirt before I sat back at the table. "His initials. Done with a screwdriver edge heated over the kitchen stove. It took a long time."

"Yeah," he said softly. "It would," and we sat for a minute. I don't know what he was thinking about.

Finally he stood up. "O.K., Iverson. I'm satisfied. Get your hat and let's take a walk," and I stood up, too, putting the dishes in the sink.

"Let me rinse these out first," I said. "It'll just take a second. I hate to see dirty dishes lying around."

He laughed, a harsh laugh. "Me too. I used to get so sick of a sinkful of dirty dishes that I'd wash them myself. Gets the shop grease out from under the fingernails."

For some ridiculous reason the thought of this lunk washing dishes made me feel better, and I had to smile. "You go ahead," I told him, "and I'll be right behind you. Down at the office?"

"If you want, or on the beach. The wall's all finished," with an almost boyish grin.

"A wall?"

"Well, a little more than that. Down at the beach in five, ten minutes?"

"About that," and with a careless wave he left.

Ten minutes later I sat beside him on the grass, not far from the water's edge. Offshore, beyond the wall, were boats, cruisers, outboards, canoes, rowboats, and a large houseboat with signs indicating it was Channel Two's eyes and ears.

"How do you like it?" He included the world in a sweeping gesture.

"All right, I guess," dubiously.

He was indignant. "Only all right? Hell, Iverson, we're over the hump. Solid, safe. This is Regan, and we're home free."

I said, "I thought you bought this island, that this was Regan territory."

"Sure," he said. "I bought it. But governments can change, just like people. Did you think that a pork chop would be safe in a dog pound? No, now we're safe. Safe from anything."

"Anything?"

"Anything!" He stood up and pointed at the offshore herd of boats. "Know why I'm just sitting here watching them try to figure out what happened, trying to get in? Well, because I want them to try, to know it can't be done!"

I said, "You must have been afraid of something. What are you afraid of?"

"Right now," he said triumphantly, "not a solitary thing," and I let it go at that.

It wasn't long after that I saw it from the air, and very many flights later it still was startingly impressive. The Regan machine—merry-go-round was as good a name as any—had used a standard Regan preset pattern. Generally domelike, it swooped up in places, back and forth in others, formed ogive and Gothic arches in still others, and left oddly shaped holes and grilles for ventilation, together with an unfinished top-center aperture. Made from the air and the water—and don't think *that* didn't knock DuPont and Hercules on their collective butts—it was proof against anything Regan had ever come up against. Over a certain size it was ineffective, under a certain size crowded; islands were natural bases, and salt-water islands of the proper size were few and subject to tidal forces.

The hole in the center? The vent holes? No worry; after the dome was at a certain stage in construction the lines of force were in effect all over the perimeters. What force? I had it explained to me twice and then I gave up, knowing at least as much as Captain Lukkari knew about her spaceship engines; just enough to tell her controls what to do. But it was the same force that propped up the curving-inward dome during construction that moved her cruiser KAYTA and her landing ship. I must go into that some time.

That same day I watched the merry-go-round scuttle down the wall, finish a gaping space at ground level into a tunnel-shaped arch that ended inside a short distance from the beach, outside the wall in shallow water certainly deep enough for our small hovercrafts, and collapse at our feet with a hiss and clank and slurp of its retracting tubes like a Sicilian eating vermicelli. Later on the high schoolers trundled it back into the palms out of sight, where it sat for a long time. Many times I walked over and watched it squatting there, half-expecting it to take a deep breath or maybe sneeze. There was never a speck of rust.

The dome effect ended at some feet below the dome base itself, which accounted for our water, sewage, and light not being uninterrupted; the dead telephones Jordan had turned off himself when the lights had annoyed him. When I asked what happened when some enterprising sapper dug under the dome rim, or what if the power lines or water mains were cut, he gently reminded me of the power-ball we had seen buried. Enough for a century, he said. Water? The merry-go-round converted sludge to $H_2O$, if necessary. But about digging under the dome? Sensors, he said, and anyone who tried it would lose something besides his dignity, as well as having to dig all the way from shore.

Of course, this was the standard Regan approach, the standard Regan fort, because it *was* a fort. Well, as Jordan had said, we have no weapons—only a few tools. "Isn't it, incidentally, about time you became a Regan citizen?"

A thought struck me. "Wait," I said. "When you became a Regan you had Lee Lukkari's mind jammed into yours. Does that mean—"

"Naw," he grunted. "Too complicated. You'll get the language, a general background of the Regan Group, a short history of Lee's planet—and now mine, too—all canned. Actually a broad consensus of scholarly technical texts. Computer stuff, all untouched by human hands. Why? Would you like to share memories with me or Lee?"

I shuddered. "If I had to, I think I'd back out and take my medicine."

He considered this briefly. "I suppose so," he said at last. "I wouldn't have stood still for it if I'd known what was coming. Embarrassing as all hell, the first few days. Especially when you try to sleep and so on." Then he smiled. "But once you get used to it, it's all right. It's kind of fun finding out that you know things you never thought you would. Are you all set?"

I shivered a bit. "As ready as I'll ever be," and we both stood up from the grass where we had been talking and watching. We started off together, heading for the spaceship. As we neared it, the hull section swung down, and Captain Lee Lukkari stood at the top of the ramp, just inside the ship itself. She smiled at Jordan as we came up the slope of the gangplank, and her smile was the type one saves for a particular person. She smiled at me too, a perfectly genuine smile, but it was a different type. I didn't hate her quite as much as I had. I paused at the end of the ramp, dazzled by our Peche Island sun, honestly scared almost stiff by the unknown. They saw my hesitancy, said or did nothing, making it clear they were waiting for me to make up my mind. Just like the first time off the thirty-foot board, I reminded myself, and stepped off the ramp into the ship. And the lights hurt my eyes.

A little fretfully, I'm afraid, I complained, "Do these lights have to be so bright?"

Jordan said, "What lights?"

"Why, these . . ." I was lying down. Jordan and the captain were sitting staring at me. I said sheepishly, "You slipped me a mickey."

Jordan began to laugh. "Something like that. The lights I saw were red, white, orange, and gin. Call it a mickey if you want, sugar, but it's quick and easy. If I'd seen that gadget draped over my head and the clamps and whatnot, I'd have been scared, too. So you got the same treatment I got. How do you feel?"

Before I answered I looked around the room. It looked like an ultramodern recreation room, bright colors here, subdued shades there, furniture that might have been metal or wood or anything else, and after I studied it a while I realized that it was really quite small. Jordan and Lee Lukkari were half-sitting on chairs that resembled Finnish Modern, and I was lying (I sat up quickly and adjusted my kilt height) on what seemed to be a soft sarcophagus (and that covered part of the engine that protruded up from another part of the ship).

Lee Lukkari said, "How do you feel?"

I opened my mouth to reply and then I realized she was not talking English. And I understood her. I groped for words, and they slid into my mind. "Why, all right, I think. You're not talking English!"

She smiled. "It is a surprise?"

I hunted for words again. "Why, yes, of course. I won't ask you how you did it."

"Why not?" said the captain. "This is a tool anyone can use and grasp. It is often that a first contact is reluctant, or frightened at entering my ship; once the Contact is inside—and it must be voluntary—he (or she, or it) is anesthetized, carried to your couch where you are now sitting, attachments are made, and I believe your word is bingo."

I understood her perfectly. When I tried to talk, I had to make a mental effort in my own language, visualizing that I wanted Regan words, and the needed vocabulary slid to my tongue. I understand this is common for one unfamiliar with a foreign language. I tried to explain my reactions, and Jordan was unsympathetic.

"You'll get over that if you talk nothing but Regan

for a few days," he said. "Your accent is lousy right now; I can tell, and I still don't talk as well as I'd like to."

"True," agreed the captain. "Dana Iverson, suppose you try to speak our language and I will use yours. We both need the practice, I think."

"All right with me," I said, a little thickly. "Could I get down off this coffin lid?"

Jordan came over and helped me to a reclining chair. "Just take it easy for a while. Don't let your tongue get mixed up with two languages. You got a headache?"

I had, at that. Lee Lukkari stood up, made gestures to open a hidden wall shelf, and I crunched between my teeth the tiny capsule she handed me. It had a neutral taste, and my headache said goodbye. She turned to Jordan, who got up with a "See you later," and started out. He also made the right gestures, and when the wall irised open I could see the gangplank leading to the outside, and the bright sun shining before the wall closed.

Lee Lukkari said, "I believe you expect me to ask you how it feels to be a Regan. So how does it feel to be a Regan?"

For a moment I resented that half-smile of hers, and then I managed an answering smile and then we were laughing together; me more in relief now that I'd burnt my bridges than anything else. After a few mutual snickers that eventually turned into ha-has she stood up and stripped off her clothes, tossing them on her chair. She scratched the usual places happily. "It feels so much better.... Don't you want—no, you are accustomed to wearing these confining garments. We are alone now, you realize."

I made up my mind all at once. While she was getting her shoes off and scratching her ankles I tossed off my blouse, stepped out of my skirt—and that's as far as I got, but I did wiggle around and unhook the bra two notches. The shoes I used my toes to slip off. I had to stare at the captain's cleanly naked body, and she looked up.

"You are curious about something. You have a question?"

I gulped. "Your body. . . ."

She turned around solemnly for my inspection. "Yes?"

I said "Your hair. . . ."

"Yes?"

I said, "Your hair . . . under the arms, I know. But on your body, between your legs . . . Is this natural?"

"Of course not," she said instantly. "Cosmetics, you call them. Remove hair from where it is not wanted—I see what you mean. No, on my planet body hair is regarded as animal-like, or at least unclean. Cosmetics? Did you think I was born with red lips and rosy cheeks and wavy hair? Hah! I spend as much time primping—primping?—as you do, but only when I wish to change my appearance or style. When Ken Jordan and I chose this costume for Regans on your planet I had much difficulty finding the way I wished my hair to appear, for one example. My personal machine—you have no word for it" (it was *kutraimi*, my mind told me) "repairs my face and hair when it is needed. I do not yet read your language as easily, as the letters are much different from mine, and it is much harder to use my eyes together with my mind. But I have read many of your magazines, and watched many of your broadcasts, and it is of much amusement to me to note all these lipsticks which are permanent—permanent until they are touched."

She was eager, interested as much in my reactions as in her own words. "Permanent? Hah! I show you 'permanent'," and she tugged me only too easily into another compartment. It was an odd-looking bedroom to me. She said, "You like your color lipstick? Lighter? Darker?" while she poked at shelves and lockers that emerged in series from the walls. "Here," she commanded, "remove your old cosmetic," and I used the tinted vial she handed me, with my own tissues taken from my purse, which I still gripped (while clad only in panties and bra, which ought to prove something).

When the old lipstick was scrubbed away, she handed me a slim tube of color almost exactly like our own Earth lipstick. "Use this," she said. "It is as close to your old shade as I have." A soft-lighted mirror swung down from the wall. When I was through she demanded, "This looks the way you want it to?" I checked again from all angles, didn't like one edge, and redid it. "You are satisfied? Good!" She came up with another vial. "Put this one on. No, right over your lips, do not rub, that's right. . . . Now, this is the permanent lipstick of my Regan Group. Something less to carry," and I remembered the tiny case she had flicked off her upper thigh a few minutes before.

"Permanent?" I said doubtfully.

"Permanent," she said emphatically. Then she reconsidered. "At least—I divide in my head—at least seven, eight of your months."

Oh, baby, I thought to myself, would this be a—hey, did I have to wear this exact shade for seven, eight months?

"Why not?" but then she came up with a different-shaped container. "Removes immediately. Put on another. Here," and she dropped a handful of tubes in my hand. "Different colors. Try them all if you like. Sit down, here, in the next compartment," waving her hand, poking invisible switches, and chairs and a bed emerging from the floor, "or lie down and rest." Apologetically: "Your clothes make me itch and sweat. I bathe while you rest," and one wall flipped out and she stepped into a girl-sized compartment. Almost immediately it opened again and her head stuck out. "You think of questions while you wait," and she was gone again. I walked back to the other room (although my head supplied the stubborn word "compartment") and leaned back in Jordan's vacant seat. With so many questions to ask where should I start?

It took all of the afternoon, a slice of the evening, and I ended by broiling Delmonicos in my kitchen for the three of us. I learned much I wanted to know, some things I hadn't wanted to know, and just enough to solidly gel my somewhat shaky convictions that I had done the right thing. I looked forward to being well over a hundred years old.

The next morning we went to New York.

# Chapter Fifteen

The assembly hall was full, as it always was when Jordan showed up. Lee Lukkari left immediately for Switzerland to pick up our gold, leaving Jordan and myself to face the UN assemblage. (I noted that the descent and takeoff from the UN Plaza was causing less and less turmoil with every visit.) Jordan said the customary words of greeting while I sat alongside him, quite uncomfortable at the eyes staring at me; it was the first time Jordan had ever appeared with anyone else besides the captain. The United States ambassador recognized me at once, as enough newspapers and magazines had carried my picture together with as much data as could be excavated. Why had Jordan picked as assistant an ex-secretary, an ex-barmaid, and all that sort of thing? I suppose there were quite a collection of dossiers concerning me.

Without warning, Jordan had me stand in the limelight to make me repeat the formula for Regan citizenship he had gone through with his captain. Looking at the "United States of America" plaque almost in front of me gave me a momentary twinge, and the look on the face of the ambassador as I stood up to calmly discard my national heritage was almost physical pain. But I said my say, and sat down, watching the American ambassador speak shortly and fiercely to one of his aides.

Jordan thanked everyone politely, sat down. The expression on his face said very plainly, any questions?

The American ambassador had one. "Can we discuss this rather flexible matter of obtaining Regan Group citizenship?"

Jordan said, "If you like, sir. But this is an established precedent of this council; my Regan Group citizenship was handled exactly the same way, here in the same place. Rather flexible? I am not sure I understand your phrase."

The ambassador said, "Mrs. Iverson—"

"Dana Iverson. No title."

"Dana Iverson. A citizen of the United States one instant, and of your Regan Group the next. No training, nor probationary period—it was mentioned that before you, Ken Jordan, became a Regan, you had to obtain a background of language, of history, of customs. Instant knowledge, so to speak."

Jordan's smile was politely angelic. "That's right, sir. Dana Iverson has all this."

In open disbelief, the ambassador snapped, "Another case of what has been called 'squeezed-in' minds? Oh, come now—"

"Not at all, sir." Damn, this Jordan could be polite when he wanted to be. "Nothing involving personalities; just knowledge. Instant knowledge, if you like those words. Language, history, customs, habits, the works. Yesterday afternoon, if you're curious."

There was a short silence while the connotations of this sunk in. This, then, meant that anyone, any time, might be the next Regan citizen. Who's next for the lottery? In the tumult that followed, Jordan spoke to me in Regan.

"I think the Russians are too happy. I think they're going to blow what you called your cover," and I looked at the Russian group leader. He did have a smirk on his face.

Jordan said, "I believe this gentleman from the U.S.S.R. has a statement, or a question?"

You bet he did. He said, "May I ask your Dana Iverson a few questions?" Without waiting for an answer he swung his glare at me. "Why is it, Dana Iverson, that you alone have won the confidence, shall we say, of Ken Jordan enough so that you have been chosen as a member of his Regan Group?"

I glanced at Jordan, got the go-ahead, and said, "Are you familiar with the jobs I have had, say, over the past ten years?" From the surge of triumph that said yes yes YES through the little wafer in the case on my right thigh I got my answer. The Russian knew!

I said, "I have had many jobs, starting with office work, with which I am very familiar. I am familiar with buying, with personnel, with office and printing equipment; my background, with a touch of natural vanity, is much wider and more varied than that of the average woman of my age. Ken Jordan has complimented me on the quality of my work."

The Russian had me where he wanted me. "Can you tell us then, Dana Iverson, how you of all women, even with these varied talents, managed to contact and be hired by Ken Jordan? And how did you, at twenty-nine years, manage to have all the opportunities to work at all these different jobs?"

Ho, boy. I thought of Mac, my government boss rotting away at a desk in Rock Island or ATAC or air base someplace; I could see Farber, *his* boss, explaining helplessly in turn to *his* boss. But this was what Jordan wanted, what my own conscience—twisted or not—told me was right.

"This is very simple, sir," I replied. "These jobs were all temporary, but at each one I learned a lot. As for obtaining them, no trouble there. They were obtained, in some cases created for me, as useful and necessary camouflage for my real function as an employee of the Central Intelligence Agency of the government of the United States." I heard the great collective gasp and gave them time to take it in, "from which I have resigned to become a Regan citizen."

The Russian, robbed of his planned climax of exposure, sat down and the American ambassador put his head in his hands. With all the dirty linen out where everyone could see it, there was a lot of commotion, all boiling down to the single fact there was a squealer, a rat, on the premises. The guiding principle behind intrigue at international levels is don't get caught, but if you do we never knew you. I sat there with Jordan, and I felt very uncomfortable. When a tall, lanky delegate from the Commonwealth managed to get the floor there was real venom in his voice and disgust in his face.

"Then I understand," he said clearly and coldly, "that you have traded your nation's welfare—if what you say is true—for the advantages of another more remote future?"

"No sir," I said at once. "I was offered Regan citizenship freely, with no reward above that of being a Regan. As for my CIA career, Ken Jordan was always aware of my double standard, long before I knew of it myself, or my supervisors. I traded no information, no data, I gave nothing except good honest work and I expect to do nothing more. No bribes, no offers, no deals."

He went a little too far. He not only did not believe a word I'd said, but he stared at me up and down, at my kilts and legs and my body, managing to show me he thought I was a high-class call girl, that I'd traded sex for security. Oh, he was blatant, and I didn't like it one bit. He said, oh so politely, "Your talents *are* rather obvious, Dana Iverson. Alien citizenship is, perhaps, a fitting reward."

A little imp inside me said to let 'em have it. I smiled as though his words had been compliments. "Thank you, sir! But I think you have misunderstood. It is not usual to have sexual dalliance, if that is what you're referring to, with someone who falls asleep on the living room floor and snores," which Ken had done the night before while Lee Lukkari and I were still talking.

Ken Jordan coughed, shot me an angry—panicky!—look, and there was a snort of amusement in the background, which turned into a general round of guffaws. Sex is rather funny when one talks about it openly.

There was a short recess. I ducked into the ladies' room, wiggled my way in and out and away from everyone I could, staying as close as I could to Jordan just on general principles, and when the session resumed tried to hold my skirts at a dignified level and my knees close together.

Jordan spent most of the remaining time explaining about the dome that he'd erected around his island. He stated flatly that it was defensive, a protection against thugs who might want to steal his gold, which was now on the way there.... On the way? Sure, Lee Lukkari was at the minute reloading in Switzerland. And what was the Regan Group going to buy? He'd know better in a week or so, and plans were already in progress.... An afternoon of this, and I was glad when it broke up. We rode via commercial air back to Detroit; Jordan said at this stage we'd be a lot safer alongside a planeload of passengers. We got an Avis car at Detroit Metro, called ahead to have one of our hovercrafts meet us at the C & O docks, and scooted into our protective dome close to dusk. I gave the hovercraft pilot ads to put in the papers calling our employees back to work and went in to call WLDM to find out what records had been played at 3:38 P.M. on the nineteenth and at 7:26 P.M. on the twenty-second. Then I had cheese and crackers and a beer and went to bed. When I turned out my bedroom light I could see light streaming out the windows of the German-style bar on the far corner. Ken Jordan was apparently not sleepy yet.

The two records, incidentally, turned out to be antiques. One was from the early 1930s and one from the forties: "Variations on Pop Goes the Weasel," by the Carnegie Pops Orchestra, and "Ma, He's Making Eyes At Me," sung by one Beatrice Kay. For a new disc of each, pressed from the gold master, Jordan paid well over three million dollars; not all at once, but during the next few years. It seems that Lee Lukkari had heard them both, liked them, and based on the frequency of play throughout the Regan Group and the standard ASCAP fee, had come up with this astonishing figure, which the original recording firms accepted with stunned thanks. This explained why Ken Jordan had always kept an FM radio within arm's reach of him. Word of this leaked out, of course, and no one will ever know how many composers came up with various tonal combinations to try to sell to Regan. Very few made it.

The high schoolers dribbled back to work the next morning on the hovercrafts, and the older employees;

everyone took his or her turn marveling at the protective dome, and I gave up trying to keep some kind of order when Lee Lukkari's spaceship dropped down through the central hole in the dome and began to methodically disgorge blocks of gold covered with thick elastic protective covering. One at a time, the blocks dropped haphazardly off the gangplank, with the hull opening and closing like the gill of a great fish. As each block hit the ground it thunked solidly into the grass, and the spaceship shifted and swung slightly until the blocks were scattered over a block-square area.

"You're not going to leave them there like that?" I asked Jordan, who was standing watching the unloading and the high schoolers with equal enjoyment.

"Nope," he said. "Let's see how smart these kids are. Order some pinchbars, some chain, some two-by-sixes, and an A-frame; pick out some huskies and tell them where you want them piled."

"What's an A-frame?" I wanted to know.

He laughed. "Ask the kids, and if they're smart enough they'll tell you," and he walked away. He was right, and in two weeks and much commotion the blocks were stacked neatly, exactly where I wanted them.

It was surprising to find out at first hand how valuable the Burns guards, now dismissed, had been. People of all shapes and sizes, mostly salesmen but some curiosity hunters, kept trying to get onto the island. The water inside our entrance was too shallow for anything but our hovercrafts or a rowboat, but people kept coming until in desperation—and this on the very first day—I placed several ex-footballers at the entrance with orders that no one, *no one*, come ashore that did not arrive on one of our hovercrafts. A telephone call to our hovercraft dock took care of the other end; clearance from me or Jordan was necessary before leaving the dock. Nothing took care of the enterprising individuals who paddled their canoes or rowboats right into our entrance; they kept coming and getting turned away. When the sightseeing girls in shorts appeared, as they did very shortly, I had to reinforce the footballers with some of our own girls to keep their minds on their work. It worked reasonably well.

Just before the spaceship left, Jordan came in with Lee Lukkari and a map. He spread it out on my desk. "Here," and he pointed.

"Shallow water," I agreed. "OK with the Canadians?"

"Everything set. I cleared that when I bought our island. Lee's leaving now."

I looked up at her. "Right now?"

She nodded. "Now, or in a few minutes. Why?"

I hesitated. "Oh, nothing too important."

She looked at Jordan. "Say goodbye now, Ken. Dana Iverson will walk me out to the ship."

He shifted uncomfortably. "OK. Well, goodbye, then," and for an instant his hand moved as though to touch her. But he changed his mind and said again, "Goodbye," and walked out.

I got up from my desk and followed Lee Lukkari out the door. It was warm outside, almost too warm, with the sun beating down through the dome. The spaceship was sitting over in the center of the island, and we started toward it, walking slowly together.

She said, "You have a question."

"I don't know," I said slowly. "Maybe it's a question, maybe it's something I should understand and don't. Maybe it's just none of my business."

We walked a few paces further. "Yes?" she said.

"All right," and I came out with it. "A few days ago you came over to see me. I got mad," and she smiled faintly. "You as much as told me you can't get along without Ken Jordan, because you have him inside you; you as much as told me he can't get along without you. Isn't that right?"

We kept walking. "Yes," she admitted. "I can't get along without him. This is due to my training; even if he were an entirely different person I would still feel that way. I shall be a very incomplete person without him—without a mind interchange, you cannot know just how incomplete, unfinished, lonely, or any word you choose."

"I think I can try," I said. "A hole where your heart ought to be, is one way of putting it."

"More than that. A hole where *everything* ought to be."

"OK," I said. "But this I don't understand—why did you tell me all this? *Me*, and at the time all you knew was that I was a spy? Or for that matter, why tell me at all?"

We drifted to a stop, and she reached to pick up a clover bud. "Several reasons, Dana Iverson. One was that, as a spy, you were certainly expected to use your physical charms, if you thought it necessary."

"Yes," I said. "Yes. It's been known to happen."

She went on quietly. "You are very attractive. Is there a better way to anger an attractive woman than to remind her how soon, how inevitably, she will lose that attractiveness? That was the tactic I used."

"Your training?"

"My training. It was very thorough. . . . Another reason? Women, men, people, are basically alike. Wherever they live, whatever they look like, modified only by conditions. Is it so shameful for one woman to tell another that she wants this man and no other?"

"This is the part I don't understand," I burst out, and she interrupted me.

"Ken right now wants no one. Not even with himself is he happy or comfortable. This is not good, but it is true, it is inevitable. It will be some time before he takes any interest in any woman, because now he feels inferior. Inferior? Yes, that is the word. Because he now has softness, gentleness, femininity inside him, he feels inferior. He is wrong, but he feels inferior. It will be quite some time before my personality is submerged in his; his personality has already surmounted mine. This is where you come in, Dana Iverson."

"Me?"

"You. I will not always be around. You will. Ken Jordan now thinks too much like me; eventually he will think like Ken Jordan, with Lee Lukkari in the background where she belongs. He will be attracted to you. What better person to be attracted to than a fellow Regan?"

We started walking again. I said, a little bitterly, "You must have been sure I'd become a Regan. You must have been sure I'd jump when you pushed the right buttons. This marvelous training, I suppose." She said nothing, and we were now close to the ship.

"So you set me up for a patsy, a sitting duck. So you schedule Ken Jordan to wake up and fall for me just like that? So suppose I don't want him? Or suppose I get him before you do, and suppose I decide to keep him? Where does that leave you?"

"Where does that leave me?" she said softly. "Exactly where I am now."

We were alongside the ship and the gangplank dropped. I watched her walk up, and at the top, just inside the ship, she turned around as the gangplank swung back up and I turned away. When I next looked in that direction, the spaceship had gone.

## Chapter Sixteen

Roosting on your own island has definite advantages, but it irks the press no end—especially when the boats they hire to get to you are turned away, when persistence on the telephone earns them only a sore ear, when helicopters cannot drop through what is obviously a widely gaping entrace in a dome. The press tried darkness as a mask; they were much annoyed when electric eyes across our main (and only) entrance waked our young football huskies. At that hour of the morning the huskies were angry.

Therefore the press was pleasantly surprised when Jordan invited ten—no more, including cameramen—to his open-for-business open house. I composed the letters that invited some very prominent businessmen, together with their legation commercial attachés, if they had one. Everyone showed up at our hovercraft dock on Riverside Drive early on the appointed date; the Burns men combed out the phonies on Canadian soil, and the biggest high schoolers on our island were very energetic about removing the ones that got by. I was inwardly amused at how easily I caught two myself at our entrance. Acting as hostess alongside Jordan, it was no trouble at all: You are Mr. Van Hootekamp? *No*, from the wafer. Out!

Everyone lollygagged around, properly amazed at our dome, at the pretty girls with the short kilts, and the luxurious living pattern we showed them. (One of our girls came over to warn us that one gentleman was down at the far end of the island trying to chip a piece off our wall. Jordan grinned, and sent her back with a hammer and chisel.) All four of our bars were fluid with freeloaders, our cooks and waitresses served food out in the open (with no worry of rain, why not?), and after everyone was seated our electronic whizkids set up and rolled the PA system. Jordan started to talk.

"There's no need for you, gentlemen, and you, ladies, to worry about taking notes. Each of you will be furnished with a tape of everything said here as you leave. So relax. If you want anything our crew can get you, stick up your hand and signal. OK?

"OK. Some of you are quite well known in the business field; some of you are not. But what I am going to say applies to everyone. There can be, will be, no exceptions.

"There has been some discussion about what the Regan Group really wants here. The answer is very simple. This is our outpost, where we buy what we want—not what we need, because our purchases are frankly luxury items—and pay for it in real value acceptable to anyone. Some of you represent companies and brand names known throughout the world; some of you don't, and this is no coincidence. Each of you represents a possible source for items we will buy. If you meet our requirements, which may or may not be rigid depending on your ideas, we can do business."

This was the talk merchants liked to hear. Everyone was on the edge of his seat.

"I'm clear so far?"

A murmur of agreement.

"I want certain items. I want the best available. I will pay not only a reasonable price, I will pay a good price. I will take delivery of practically any available quantity, just a few short miles from here. I will pay in gold upon delivery. Yes?"

A redfaced man asked where, a few miles from here.

"In Canadian waters, too shallow for ordinary navigation, courtesy of the Government of Canada. Delivery and loading into barges, or lighters, I think they are called. I must repeat this statement; I must have the exact quality of anything I intend to purchase. There can be no 'export quality,' no substitutions, no put-it-on-the-bottom-row. Everything I buy will be shipped a distance so enormous I still don't believe it myself."

This earned a polite chuckle. Hell, I still couldn't comprehend the distance to the Regan Group myself.

"You may think I'm a little too extreme about quality. Gentlemen, I'm an old shop hand, I know all about quality: this business of making things just good enough to get by the inspectors, making things to high tolerance because it costs money to adjust the machines, goofing off and burying the goof down in the bottom because statistical quality control says the last ten orders were OK so why not this one! Quality control is just a word, just a janitor who now is a maintenance engineer. I want inspection. I want inspectors! I don't want spot checks that let borderline junk slip through for the poor goat out in the field. If the items call for one hundred percent inspection, that's what I want. I'm willing to pay for it.

"You know something else? I don't sign contracts. If you put what I want at my door I'll buy it. I'll keep buying it. Even if you get careless, or even get slippery with one shipment, I'll still buy it. And you know what I'll do with it? I'll dump it right in the deepest part of the ocean, with your national flags painted all over it, and I'll hire every cameraman I can find to take pictures of the junk sinking. Get me a beer, will you sugar?"

I signaled a waitress, and he drank a pint in a gulp.

"Now you know why I asked your group or government representatives to be here. As a man who was born and raised on Earth, I don't want myself to be the one who has to say, 'Earth was my home planet, and I didn't know it was junk when I shipped it.' And if you gentlemen—and ladies—have any national or group pride, you will want to take steps to see that this pride filters down the line to the worker who is going to see his product go to the stars."

Very poetic, hey? Jordan could forget his shop dialect when he wanted to. With Lee Lukkari's mind in his, her wider vocabulary had driven him to reading the dictionary when he thought I wouldn't notice. The words in my mind—and there were a lot of them—that had no Earthly equivalent, I just forgot. But I'd use them some day when I got home to the Regan Group. Home, in the Regan Group. A funny word, that 'home.'

A hungry-looking man stood up.

"You are saying, I take it, that this first contact, as you called it at the United Nations in New York, is only a commercial venture." I couldn't see his name on his yellow ticket—press. Jordan had asked me why I'd specified yellow tickets, but I hadn't told him.

"Why, sure," Jordan said. "Commercial as hell. Commercial like Columbus looking for gold in the

East, like Magellan looking for a shortcut to spices he could buy and resell. Uh-uh, hold it, I'm not finished. With this exception: Magellan's boss didn't care much about the natives he met, and Queen Isabella of Spain didn't either. My bosses do. We take nothing, we rob nobody. We trade to make a profit, so other cruisers can go out and explore. You got anything against making a profit?"

Again, very choice words. Who can honestly say he doesn't want to make a profit? The hungry type sat down.

Jordan took a deep breath. "That's about it. I know this is practically unheard of in the business world, this insistence on perfection. So why not take a couple of weeks to think it over? Go back home, consult with your engineers, your wholesalers, your political leaders, and come back and tell me what you intend to do. If you decide the requirements are too stiff, no hard feelings, as my plans are always elastic." He sat down.

The crowd, which must have numbered over a hundred, just sat there uncomfortably while Jordan beamed impartially all around. Nobody wanted to lead with his chin. A young, stagy-looking Englishman stood up, and it was Wolfie, my Swiss introduction to Jordan's bank account.

"Sir!" he said. "Ken Jordan!"

Jordan lazily stood. "You have a question?"

"No, sir!" Wolfie was strong for his country, and strong in his voice. "As commercial attaché, I represent the government of Switzerland. There is nothing we Swiss cannot make, nothing we cannot produce, to the highest standards possible. Our nation of skilled workmen challenges the world. We accept one hundred percent terms. We welcome them!"

A darkskinned man was on his feet in a flash. His

country was ready. The Russian who had challenged me at my appearance at the UN roared out from the back of the crowd, and in two seconds so had everyone else. (The Russian I'd met at the island entrance. He'd denied he was secret police, but my wafer had just snickered at the "commercial attaché." And the dinner date I'd promised Wolfie, the Swiss, for being first on his feet would *not* be on his oh-so-fast Swissair jet, but on our own island, a date you can walk home from.)

Ken Jordan stood patiently, letting the national zeal burn itself out. At last, long after the Russian was hoarse, he said happily, "Gentlemen, you have reacted exactly as I hoped you would. You wish, instead of waiting for a later date, to talk business immediately. Right now!" It was obvious they did. He beamed at them.

"If you gentlemen will turn over your plastic name badges you will find a tiny number on the back." He watched while everyone at once fumbled at his lapel, some ripping materials in their eagerness. "You all have seen the numbers? Now, somewhere back of that row of palm trees—any of our girls will show you where—there will be a big table and easy chairs and cold drinks and a very knowledgeable buyer who will describe fully, and in some cases, show you physically what we Regans wish to buy. So there will be no misapprehension, you will be furnished a transcription of what our buyer states, and your replies. Take these with you when you leave, for study for your bids. I need not tell you secrecy between bidders is not necessary, as each of you will be asked to bid on a different item. So, gentlemen, ask the girl in the kilts at the end of your row to escort you to our buyers. If you want anything, there will be a young lady there to see you get it.

"One more thing, gentlemen. Closed or sealed bids are not needed and not wanted. I think two weeks should be enough for your companies or your groups to prepare a bid. You do, too? Thank you," and he hopped down from his tiny dais, ducking the ones that tried to buttonhole him, heading for my office.

We got there together, and I gave the high schoolers on door-duty the signal that meant no visitors. Then I opened the door to hold up the two fingers that meant beer. He brought it in very quickly and I opened both bottles. Dortmunder is good, but rough on the kilt size.

"What are you thinking about?" I asked curiously.

Jordan smiled ruefully. "Lots of things. Like what France is going to say when I buy Australian wines."

Yes, I'd thought of that. "But you *like* Australian wines."

"Not me," he denied instantly. "I like the hard stuff, or I used to," he amended sadly. "Now I stick to beer. . . . No, it's Lee Lukkari's taste that likes Australian wines. I wouldn't know one wine from another. I even bought her some Australian wine and some French wine from a Canadian liquor store. But she likes the Australian wine better, and it's going to make a lot of Frenchmen unhappy."

"Quien sabe?"

"What's that mean?" suspiciously.

"It means, who knows? It also infers, who cares?"

"Quien sabe?" he repeated. "Yeah." He heaved himself out of the chair. "One of the girls said she saw the Russian trying to snip off a piece of our merry-go-round. Secret police, hey?" I nodded. He chuckled softly. "Secret, hey?" He left.

In hours and days, the bids started coming back; the first few I was curious about, and consulted one of

Jordan's commercial buyers. With the red veins in his nose and upper cheekbones, it was certain that he knew more about whiskey than Jordan.

"You think there's a mistake in this bid for Irish whiskey?" he said. "Dana Iverson, it's a good thing *you* aren't buying it in the lots that Ken Jordan wants. Did you know that right now in Hong Kong, halfway across the world from the North Sea, you can buy the best Scotch or Irish for a dollar a bottle? And everyone that handled that bottle made money on it! Of course," he added honestly, "That's a fifth—not imperial quarts."

"Then why—" I started to say.

"Hah!" He knew what I was going to ask. "Taxes! Every government in the world makes more in taxes than the original distiller makes in profit. You got a bid in for cigarettes? Not yet? Well, wait till you find out what you can buy cigarettes and cigars for, without taxes. Makes you think how rough things are for the average working man," he added moodily. Then he brightened. "Of course, everybody knows cigarettes aren't good for you. . . ."

In less than a week all bids were in. The buyers were unanimously sure that each bid should be driven down, but Jordan reminded them gently of his insistence on quality and let the bids stand as they were. "One thing," he said. "You are each responsible for your shipments. You're all, or most of you, leaving for the source. You can't check everything, and you're not supposed to even try. I've got a bunch of youngsters hanging around here who are getting bored. I'll give each of you a few to break in as inspectors. Tell them, show them what to look for, and send them back when you think they'll be helpful; send them back certainly by fall, because they'll be going to college off and on." We'd set up quite a complicated school attendance schedule already. "Now, you're all experts in your fields. Each of you should be able to smell trouble, even if you can't spot it. Anything like that, get in touch with me at once, and I'll come out in the field and find the missing link for you. And you've been told about bribes; go ahead, take them, and then tell me and I'll match the bribes again as part of your salary. Bribes don't bother me—it's what they try to cover with a bribe that interests me. Go to it."

In two days, the buyers and half the high schoolers were gone, some by commercial air, and the rest in shuttle trips in Jordan's jet which had been sitting unused since its latest overhaul. I checked again on the progress of the aluminum lighters being assembled in New Brunswick, bought the old *City of Tashmoo* less engine and upper works, and anchored the lovely, lonely old girl's hull off Belle River, in the center of the weedbeds in water so shallow the towing tug had trouble spotting her. The first load of Irish whiskey was being loaded in Dublin, and we needed container space.

Optimism was up so high in the export business that it took rather longer than we expected to get international fireworks. Queerly enough, it was not the wire services nor the financial magazines but the Royal Oak, Michigan *Tribune* that called me to ask when we were going to advertise for bids again. I told him never, quite probably, unless someone goofed up on our present orders. He asked if we'd tell him what we were buying; I think he was planning a feature article on things the Regans bought, and consequently analyzing how they lived. I called Jordan in on the line, who promptly invited him for lunch and dinner, which was some sort of a news-beat itself. When our hovercraft took the *Tribune* man back to the Windsor shore, he carried an itemized list of everything we had on order—and the sources. There never was a feature story. But was there a feature!

The whole front page of the next day's *Tribune* carried the copyright note that newspapers use when they get somewhere first. I Xeroxed the whole front page while the ink was fresh.

It itemized our orders one by one, in a slightly different format. Columns one and two named the item; columns three and four, the sources; columns five and six, the comments. Interested in the list, and the comments?

*FOODS*

| | | |
|---|---|---|
| Coffee | Ecuador<br>Columbia<br>Ethiopia | *Not* from Brazil, producers of 90% of the world's coffee. |
| Tea | China<br>Burma | From a Communist nation, and a possible Communist satellite. |
| Candy | Holland | *Not* from France, not from England, and *not* from the United States, which produces more than the rest of the world together. |
| Marmalade | British West Indies | *Not* from California, *not* from Florida oranges. |
| Cheese | France<br>Norway<br>Sweden | Not Swiss cheese, and *not* from Wisconsin, the dairy capital of the world. |
| Olives | Spain | *None* from California, the land of the super-colossal olives. |
| Spices | Asia | None from our good neighbor to the South; no chile peppers. |

| | | |
|---|---|---|
| Anchovies | Portugal | Are not American fishermen and canneries not the most efficient in the world? |
| Bacon | Denmark | *Not* from the United States; not from Texas, for example, nor Iowa, nor Kansas, nor any other state. |
| *LUXURIES* | | |
| Whiskey | Ireland | *None* from America, the home and the origin of bourbon, the finest whiskey in the world. |
| Beer | Germany | *None* from Wisconsin, *none* from Missouri, *none* from New York or Michigan. |
| Cigarettes | Bulgaria<br>Greece<br>Turkey | *None* from the United States of America, whose gentle climate and fertile soil produces cigarettes sold all over the known world at a premium. |
| Cigars | Cuba | None from Puerto Rico, and it is a known fact that Cuba's tobacco fields have never recovered from the blight of the last decade. |
| Wines | Australia | None from France, Germany, or Austria, and *none* from the great wine-producing states of Ohio, New York, or California. |

| | | |
|---|---|---|
| Rum | British West Indies | *None* from Puerto Rico, and *none* from the Virgin Islands, together producers of 75% of the world's rum. |

*MATERIALS*

| | | |
|---|---|---|
| Furs | Russia<br>Canada<br>Alaska | Only 10% of the total from American soil, and that small share to be handled by the Hudson's Bay Company, a foreign concern. |
| Wood | Africa<br>South America<br>Central America | Exotic woods, beautiful possibly, but *nothing* of the sturdy oak, ash, hickory or the valuable towering redwood of which we now have so little left. |
| Silk | China | A product of handwork by slave labor of a Communist country; *none* of our fantastic synthetics which have long ago driven silk off American shelves. |
| Linens | Belgium | *None* of the cotton of the American South that makes possible inexpensive and surprisingly rugged and dainty novelties. |
| Worsted | Scotland | *None* from America. |

| *MANUFACTURED PRODUCTS* | | |
|---|---|---|
| Carvings, sculptured art | Finland<br>Africa | *None* from the United States. Can one really believe we have no art, no creative talent, no techniques? |
| Music Boxes | Austria<br>Switzerland | *None* from the *shops* of New Jersey, *none* from the workers of New York or Delaware or Ohio. *None* from the nation that developed new materials, new techniques to make the modern music box inexpensive enough for any child to have at least one! |
| Toys | Japan<br>Hong Kong | *None* from any of the fifty-one states! *None* from the nation that personalized Santa Claus, that leads the world in the immense assortment of sturdy, inexpensive gifts for children of all ages. |

This was only the beginning of the *Tribune*'s philippie. The sale of automobiles, that particular year, was low, and with Michigan factories idling at minimum production the *Tribune* mentioned the thousands of "highly trained, high-volume" mechanics that would be oh, so valuable in manufacturing anything needed by the Regan Group.

*Time* and *Business Week* grudgingly gave the

*Tribune* credit for its copyrighted feature, and with their larger, more expert staffs, had no trouble uncovering the stunning fact that not one company, large or small, that had been invited to bid on Regan contracts was an American-owned firm. The companies with names familiar throughout the States were subsidiaries of foreign-owned concerns; all gravy, hence, would be siphoned into un-American pockets, a completely un-American activity. The business wails turned into sullen growls, rumbling from down East and inching through the Midwest. From business to emotion was an inevitable step, and quite soon Jordan was being castigated for being a traitor, for being a turncoat poltroon, and for not carrying nepotism as far as the usual businessmen or politicians. What the press said about me wasn't too bad, at first.

In a poker game, when one is dealt an ace, a pair of queens and two treys, one does not accuse the dealer of dealing seconds. It doesn't work that way in politics. The Brazilians forgot that a good portion of the exotic woods we were scheduled to buy would come from the Amazon watershed; they wanted, also, to sell us coffee. China, selling silk and part of the tea, wanted to sell us all the tea and to hell with Burma, who was an American satellite. The British West Indies, besides limes, wanted to peddle their other tropical fruits; Australia, not flattered at all by selling its wines, had millions of pounds of wool that was far better than that from the British Isles; the French Roquefort exporter, with a bellyful of cheap vin blanc, knew his brother's champagne was the best in the world, and what was wrong with cognac? Norway was sore because we wanted no lutefisk, Denmark was angry—in a typically polite Danish fashion—that we had picked Dortmunder instead of Tuborg, Löwenbräu and all of Bavaria was mad at everyone, and in general the most vituperation spilled out of the nations that were going to sell us nothing at all. (No Gorgonzola, no slivovitz, no dice; the Russians took it very hard because we wanted no caviar.) The most violent of all reactions came from a country split on social and religious lines; the north of Ireland, immensely angry because we were buying Corkonian not-a-drop-is-sold-until-it's-seven-years-old, broke up several hurling games (which to a Celt is equivalent to boycotting the World's Series), and it was rumored that retired Bushmillian Ulstermen were training a skin diver group to hang limpet bombs on outward-bound Eire cargo ships. The Netherlands, Switzerland, Belgium, and a few of the others took things in their stride and worked double shifts.

I said that at first the press was easy on me. This, I have a hunch, was because orders came down the line from Washington to use the soft pedal; I'd refused both by mail and by telephone to have any conversation with any United States representative, including Farber himself, on whom I was forced to hang up twice before he took the hint. Remembering that all the dislike and press furor was basically economic, lunch-pail and dollar-bill furor, and that as yet the first Eire freighter was not yet through the Welland Canal on the seaway route to Peche Island, you can imagine how I felt when the press had enough ammunition to get violently personal.

And it came with absolutely no warning.

## Chapter Seventeen

First—I laid things out on the desk before Jordan one, two, and so on—was this idea of paying our employees in gold. The Austrian mint was double-shift coining the old Franz Joseph ducat for us, each week the Bank of Montreal would send over what we needed to pay salaries and our smaller bills, and the young employees, especially, had all kinds of fun taking illegal gold coins home to their parents, or just showing them around.

The high schoolers, I told him, yesterday—payday—had their gold coins confiscated by United States Customs at the Windsor tunnel exit, giving in exchange receipts for so many ounces of gold at so much per ounce. The kids then went home with a piece of paper instead of money. That was number one.

Number two, the United States government would soon demand the gold that some of our older, cannier employees had banked in Canada, where gold was legal. Send your gold home, they would say, or when you get back there'll be trouble. This was still grapevine, but our Swiss and Canadian contacts had advance data.

Number three?

We had a lot of high schoolers working for us; some of them going home by hovercraft to Windsor, and then to Cottam or Royal Oak or Leamington or Hazel Park, and the rest staying in our two halls—barracks!—making the night garish with what passed for music. The youngest was a big-eyed brunette filly out of Sardinia by Minnesota. She'd graduated at fourteen from an East Detroit high school, had an IQ that was startling, and wanted to go to Chicago University, where you can get a degree in six months if you're smart enough. And a Windsor doctor's rabbit test was positive. By amateur dating, she was at least a month and a half pregnant.

"Who's the father?" Jordan asked at once. "The big redhead that's always hanging around her in the pool?"

The father: eighteen years old, an honor graduate headed for Syracuse U, and probably for jail.

"Do you know this is legally rape?" I said bitterly. "That poor idiot kid telephoned her mother, didn't have the nerve to face her. The mother went into hysterics, the father had a minor heart attack, he called the Detroit police, who called Windsor police, who called me. They want the girl, they want the boy's scalp, they want mine, they want yours for running a fancy cathouse."

I said a few more nasty things—pregnant, at fifteen!—and he listened carefully until I ran down. Then he said rather grimly, "Nobody gets anybody." He stood up. "The kids here now? Tell them both to hunt me up in the woods. I want them to take a walk with me."

"All right," I said sarcastically. "Take a walk. What about the gold you're paying with? What about the gold some of us have in Canadian banks?"

He stopped at the door. "Just keep paying off as you have been."

"Making an enemy of the wealthiest, heaviest armed, snootiest nation in the world?"

Before he left he said, "Yeah."

The press reaction was just what might be expected. No chaperones for the kids, proximity and propinquity being encouraged, foreign—alien!—supervision, and the cartoons, especially in the giveaway newspapers around Detroit's perimeter, showed me as a kilted procuress with thick legs. This approach was subtly fostered, and even the *Christian Science Monitor* got rough. Anything concerning the Regan Group was news: scandal, even better. The American howls grew frantic when Jordan refused to "give anybody to anybody," and the two kids huddled together desperately, pitifully, on our island until Jordan got them married without any parental consent by an nonsectarian minister imported from Madison Heights.

The bride's mother showed up for the wedding, also the groom's parents, and it was a very nice wedding with lilies and orchids and high schoolers on their very best behavior. After the wedding was over, the two newlyweds honeymooned not far from my place, and I started ordering medical equipment and expanding our tiny first aid room into a full-scale maternity ward. The two kids took to happy housekeeping—how could they miss, with no housekeeping bills?—buoyed surprisingly by the fact their baby would be a Regan by birth. They knew nothing about the Regan Group; after the rough treatment they had gotten from the American press they figured anything would be an improvement.

(Few of our high schoolers were back to work the first few days after the news of the pregnancy hit the papers; their parents, of course, had forbidden it, and it was several days after the marriage that they began to filter back. In some cases, it was the absurdly high wages their hungry parents were missing, and in others the kids slicked across the border and got to our hovercraft dock without being caught. Actually, we lost for good only one girl, whose parents moved back to Nashville. If they wanted to stay, Jordan said flatly, they could stay, and that was that. Diplomatic immunity did not soften one bit the universal condemnation in the newspapers of Detroit. The pressure through the UN from Washington went up, and Secretary Ngambi, called back from retirement, had several long talks with Jordan on our island, where Ngambi was always welcome. I sat in on none of the talks. I wasn't interested and I was too busy; with all the kids back in force, I was trying my best to see that there would be no more pregnancies, and to do it without being an obvious snoop. Who can be everywhere at once on a mile-long island? But I tried, and the kids—now being treated more like children instead of the adults they thought they were—resented it all to hell. But I stuck to trying to be a sexy den mother.)

Our first shipment, whiskey, sailed past our island with green flags flying and bagpipes screeching on the way to unload. The hulk of the *City of Tashmoo* was waiting, and although the freighter drew too much water to get near her, by telephone I cleaned out every able-bodied man from Belle River to Puce, and the transhipment of forty-ounce quarts from freighter to barge to *Tashmoo* went very well. They tell me the way the crews eyed each other for pilferage was hilarious, but nevertheless every public house from Ipperwash to Kingsville soon had Irish whiskey in the kitchen to sell on Sundays.

Just about this time, maybe spurred by the sight of

the green-flagged ship carrying the first of many loads past our island, an interview with Ken Jordan was formally requested by the mayor of Detroit, the governor of Michigan, both senators from Michigan, and the United States Secretary of Commerce. Jordan took this news with a grin, thought it over, and then astonished me by saying, "Any other senators want to come? Invite them along," so I did.

A passel—or is it a pride, or a skulk?—of electees showed up for our lawn party. As official greeter and screener, I met everyone at our entrance, identified them as being who they claimed to be, and nabbed the usual number of gate-crashers. At least two of them were FBI or CIA men; I didn't ask further. The high school footballers, augmented by Burns guards, saw that they rode back to Windsor on the hovercraft.

The meeting was very simple.

The senators wanted to know why *their* states were not selling anything to the Regan Group; the Secretary of Commerce had a chalk-talk and flashcards proving that anything needed could be had better, cheaper, and faster from the U.S.A.; the senator from Wisconsin was torn between his professed love for Milwaukee beer and Liederkranz, the only true American cheese (and, you know what, it is!); the California senator could say nothing about western-built aircraft, with Captain Lee Lukkari's ship around, but about his oranges, his lemons, and his dates, now ... He got into a hassle with the senator from Florida, and we watched the deadly polite fracas with solemn faces.

Jordan listened to everyone politely, and then gave everyone the same courteous no. Pressed to explain, he said, "Gentlemen, it's quite simple. Some people like pork chops, some people like lamb, I like beef.

Your brother likes fish but won't eat shrimp. I buy what I like, what we like, for the Regan Group. Protesting against this is like Sears Roebuck getting mad because you shop at Montgomery Ward's, or vice versa."

"Yes, but Mr. Jordan," this was the senator from North Carolina, "I happen to know for years you smoked Camels; you changed to Chesterfields, then to Benson and Hedge's. Oh, all fine cigarettes," he insisted loyally, "all good American cigarettes. But you're buying cigarettes from Europe, from Asia, and the flavor is entirely different. Not American at all. Why, Mr. Jordan, some years ago, I understand you once chewed raw tobacco, Liebermann's, made right here in your own state. Now, why would you not stick to what you know is good, instead of experimenting with foreign substitutes?"

Jordan smiled pleasantly. "I chewed tobacco for some time, untill I got married. I even dipped snuff when I was wearing a mask and milling beryllium in the shop. I must say, your agents have done their homework, sir. . . . But to answer your question.

"It is exactly what I have done, what I have experienced in the past that makes me select certain items in preference to others. Have you forgotten that I am buying for Regan tastes, Regan palates—and that I am a member of the Regan Group?"

A plump man stood up. "Ken Jordan?"

Jordan recognized him. "Yes, Mr. Washington?"

The mayor of Detroit said, "Ken Jordan, may I ask you a question that will certainly verge upon the personal? I ask this first because we are your guests, and because it may explain why we are here personally—or it may not."

"Sure," Jordan said. "Go ahead."

The mayor of Detroit stood silent for an instant.

Then: "Why, Ken Jordan, did you come back to Detroit to set up and to operate your 'trading post'? Your finances are immense, your—call it potential—is apparently unlimited. Why did you come back to the city where you were born, where you were married, yes, and divorced? Why did you come back to a state where it is unbearably hot in the summer and viciously cold in the winter?" The governor of Michigan coughed and turned red.

The mayor pushed on. "Why did you come back to Detroit when you had the world to pick from? Why did you come back here, when most nations in the world would have gladly signed over thousands of acres just for the privilege of seeing your spaceship—and your gold? Why did you come back to the river of your youth, oily and polluted, when you could have lived in the sun near the surf and the palm trees you wanted badly enough to ship halfway across the world? Why did you build your outpost where you were born and raised, and why did you build only one entrance, and that one entrance facing toward and accessible only from another nation? Why have you turned your back to your city, your state—and your country?" The mayor sat down, sweaty droplets on his dark temples.

I had never seen Ken Jordan quite so uncomfortable. It took a long time for him to answer. Finally: "Mr. Washington, you've come up with a series of questions that are very awkward to answer. But I'll try."

He hesitated again, and then went on slowly. "Detroit . . . Yes, I was born there. It's a lousy town. No," as heads jerked up, "I don't mean it quite that way. I meant that it's not pretty, like San Francisco, not rich like New York, not historical like New Orleans even though it's older. . . . It's a factory town, for working and for making things, where people work all their lives so they can move out of it, where the sidewalks roll up at night and all day Sunday. Sure, it's a lousy town, but I like it. All my life I made my living here.

"When I got picked for this job I had big ideas of coming back to Detroit with bells and banners and walking into the joints where I used to hang out and having everybody say, there's the hometown boy that made good. There are other reasons why I came back, technical reasons, but I have to admit I came back here because I wanted to; because I wanted to be a big noise where I used to be a popgun. OK.

"But I got over that. Call it growing up, call it the same as the little kid who finally gets a job in a candy store, call it a direct result of having a different type of mind blended with mine. I've been back to some of the places I wanted to go. When I wore Regan clothes I was recognized and got mobbed; when I didn't wear Regan clothes I wasn't spotted and I got treated a little better than I used to only because I had more money and bought more drinks. Like the kid in the candy shop, now this is just my job—the chocolate and the frosting isn't so important anymore. And that's why I came back to the Detroit River. That's why I came back to the river that no one has dared to swim in for forty years, where the fish can't live and my royal palms grow only because I got a trick roof over them. I thought I was coming home in a limousine."

He stood there quietly, looking at nothing in particular for a long time until the listeners began to stir. He shook off his mood.

"That takes care of one set of questions; let's get the rest. You're asking me why I don't buy American. You seem to have the idea this is just a whim of mine. It isn't. You just don't have anything to sell," and there was a sullen, quick rumble from everyone.

Jordan smiled grimly. "You don't believe me. All right, what kind of mechanical products have you got to sell to a system that builds spaceships faster and better than you can build automobiles? What mechanical gadgets can you offer to a system that builds equipment that you trust your life to, billions and billions of miles from a garage? What kind of electrical equipment can you sell me, when your own can't detect our spaceship coming or going or standing still?"

A tall, rangy, reddish man stood up. "You're buying tobacco from behind the Iron Curtain. What's the matter with American tobacco, and what's the matter with American whiskey and American wheat and American corn?"

Jordan shook his head ruefully. "Not one thing, sir. I smoked American cigarettes and drank American popskull all my life. But I'm a Regan Group citizen now, and I buy what Regan wants. Lee Lukkari's knowledge includes an extremely wide range of experiences; I tapped that knowledge to select Turkish tobacco and Irish whiskey. In our Regan Group, these tastes, these flavors are unique and desirable. American wheat, American corn? In the Regan Group we're not hungry. We have grains and cereals. We even have animals that provide hams—but not Danish bacon. You must understand, sir, among other things I am a purchasing agent, a trader."

The senator with the puffy face stood up. "You are a trader, you said. You are an industrial people, and I speak of your Regan Group?"

"Sure," Jordan said comfortably. "Some planets in our group have industry coming out their ears. Some of them don't have enough horsepower to drive an outboard—and don't want any. Is that what you mean?"

"That's what I mean," said the senator. "So if this is true, why not provide us with your technological advances instead of this sterile gold you have in such quantity?"

Jordan nodded. "Yes, it could be done. I could start with transportation. Let's say a car with, oh, let's say a few thousand horsepower, or a truck. A lifetime guarantee on engine, frame, body, and suspension. Top speed limited only by terrain. Automatic chauffeur, automatic driving. Cost, maybe forty dollars U.S.A., ready to drive. If I felt like building a power station, there'd be no smog and no cost for fuel. Laid down here in Detroit, maybe forty-five dollars. How many American-made cars would be sold if I did?

"Or how about a pocket computer with no keys, no buttons, no power supply? How about a house, furniture and all, that erects itself? This would cost about a hundred dollars in any climate. What you really want is a spaceship like ours to deliver a nice vicious nuclear bomb; with a few billion dollars for tooling they can be made like jellybeans. No, Senator ... Hoskins, I believe, I can't take responsibility for upsetting your economy. I won't sell you automobiles, and I won't sell you spaceships. But I will buy luxury items, special products, and I'll pay in cash. Gold. Dana Iverson!"

I said, "Yes?"

"Make a note to buy a Doall. When this Irish whiskey is unloaded it's got to be paid for."

"All right," I said. "What's a Doall?"

"A bandsaw. We'll have the kids cut up one of the gold blocks. Better get a cutting torch, too, with a few extra tanks of oxygen." He turned back to his guests.

"I'm very sorry, gentlemen, but we have other appointments on our schedule," which we didn't.

With the standard amount of confusion and an abnormal amount of reluctance, the conference broke up. The very last to leave, hanging back to present one more sales pitch, were the mayor of Detroit and Michigan's governor.

The governor said, "As you know, Ken Jordan, the national unemployment rate is very high right now. Detroit, the Motor City, has been hit the worst, and it's almost as bad in Flint, Saginaw, Lansing—you know your own state. Is there nothing at all you can use that we can build or make, or handle?"

Jordan hesitated. "Well . . . I could buy some cars. Would that help? OK, but I know car dealers—delivery direct from the factory. One hundred percent thousand-mile road test, one hundred percent inspection with my own inspectors. Normal dealer commissions to go to Michigan State unemployment funds. Can you handle it yourselves?"

Of course, but what kind?

Jordan hunched his shoulders thoughtfully. "Oh, the big Lincoln. Full power, all accessories. I could use a thousand, make it twelve hundred, on the button. Will you call Dana Iverson, Mr. Washington, when plans are firm?"

The mayor would call very soon, he said, and Jordan and I stood and watched the hovercraft splash away.

I said curiously, "What are you going to do with twelve hundred Lincolns?"

"Museums," he said sourly as we started walking. "What else?"

# Chapter Eighteen

Even though I knew basically what was going to happen, it was with a lot of curiosity that we all piled into the hovercrafts to watch the first load shipped out. The hulk of the old *Tashmoo* was down almost flush with the lake surface, case after case of Irish whiskey, braced and crossbraced, filling the old excursion queen. As we roared and splashed several circles around the *Tashmoo* to give our high schoolers the best look, there were only a few stray fishermen with their lines out for pickerel. Back in the wider part of the steamer channel was anchored the Irish freighter, now riding high in the water with its load transshipped. The reason for the lack of audience was that no one yet suspected the Regan method of moving bulk cargo.

The hovercraft turbines finally died to their whistling idle and we rocked gently for several minutes in the shallows until the young ones got restless and started the inevitable horseplay. On shore we could see cottagers focusing us in their lawn telescopes, and outboards and vacation cruisers began to emerge from their slips along the shore. Then the spaceship came down.

As the kids ohed and ahed it dropped directly down over the *Tashmoo* with its standard falcon-stoop, stopping just above the loaded hulk. Instantly the hull panel swung down, and from the ramp eased down a silvery ball into a metal rack that bulked slightly upward almost exactly in the center of the load. The ball was tiny, barely the size of a basket-ball. The spaceship at once fled upward a few hundred feet and remained motionless.

The kids began to get restless again, then ripples showed around the *Tashmoo* and the hulk quivered. It shook, it shuddered, it moaned and shrieked as stresses contrary to its design took effect. Then the entire ship began to emerge from the water. A nakedly obscene dowager, its patched hull plates showed as it struggled up. Around it, water poured down in sheets until the flood died to drips, and it hung there clear and free of the water, moving upward slowly.

It was tremendous, like the pictures I had seen of the old dirigibles; the spaceship was to me a familiar friend, but the sheer bulk of the suspended giant—long as a football field, a third of that wide—was a completely impossible sight. From the high schoolers there was not a sound as Ken Jordan and myself watched the rusted monstrous thing move up, up, up. Then its pace quickened, its size began to shrink in our eyes, and it raced away from us. We followed it as it went up, and as it became smaller and vanished the silence of our young passengers was as solid a tribute as could be found. When it was gone I let out my breath.

Jordan's amused eyes were on me. "Pretty impressive, the first time you see it, isn't it?"

"Yes," I said. "Even though you know what's going to happen."

He chuckled. "We'll see a lot more of that. But there

always has to be a first time. What's he want?" He pointed. Racing directly at us was a deckless Chriscraft with a lone driver waving at us and jumping with excitement. As he aimed at us he cut through the agitated water where the *Tashmoo* had been, pools still swirling and bubbling.

As he pulled alongside, Jordan motioned at our own pilot and our turbines began to whine. The crew of our hovercraft came to life, went to work, and both hovercrafts began to move in the water. For a few feet the Chriscraft moved alongside, the driver yelling and waving.

"Mr. Jordan," he was shouting. "Mr. Jordan! I'm with the Windsor *Star*. Can I talk to you a minute? Mr. Jordan, I'm with the Windsor *Star*, can I talk—"

Jordan looked questioningly at me, and I shrugged.

"Why not?" I said. "A lot of people have seen this, and there'll be a lot of questions. Why not give the kid a break on his vacation?" as he was dressed in shorts and nothing else.

Jordan motioned at his Russian pilot and the hovercraft settled back in the water. "All right," he called. "Get rid of your boat and come aboard."

The young fellow started to leap the gap between us, and then it dawned on him he'd be leaving his own cruiser unattended. It was his own boat, obviously; it was too battered to be a rental. Jordan saw his quick terror.

He got up and called for a line to be passed, and when the young man flipped him a length, knotted it expertly around our rear towing bitt. He waved at our pilot, and the engines started up again at low speed, hauling the Chriscraft gently behind as the owner hopped from his bow to our stern.

"My name's LeGault," he announced happily. "I'm with the Windsor *Star*. Gee, I'm glad you got a minute for me, Mr. Jordan." He was early twenties, excited, eager, and very nervous. I made the proper gestures and came up with three bottles of beer, an opener, and a ballpoint pen and big pad. He took the beer eagerly, the pen and the pad questioningly, and then remembered with a flush that a member of the press doesn't usually interview half naked. We moved to the stern of the hovercraft, under the awning, and sat down companionably. And the youngster, the first reporter to talk directly and personally to Jordan, got the story of his career.

Ken Jordan had been honestly puzzled. "What did you think I'd do with it? After I load a barge, would I reload it into something else? No, we drop in a self-contained power source—that was the round gadget you saw—adjust the field limits, because who wants a lot of lake water, hoist the load up with the field loose to let the water drain off, and then the word is go."

The reporter thought that over. "Well, Mr. Jordan —"

"Ken Jordan," automatically from me.

"Ken Jordan. But I understand space is cold, and not very much air. Wouldn't all those bottles freeze, and break?"

"You bet space is cold, and there's no air at all. No, the power source holds in or out whatever air, or gas, or anything else, is within its range, and supplies enough heat to replace that which leaks out, which is damned little. *Nothing* gets through a Regan shield."

"Not even a bomb, an atom bomb or something?" The reporter was incredulous.

"Nothing," Jordan said firmly. Almost whimsically he added, "And that goes for the one around my island." That would be news to everyone, and I wondered why he mentioned it at this particular time.

The reporter was properly astounded but did not

realize any deeper implications. He said, "Well, Ken Jordan, I can see how you did it, all right . . . but what happens later on?"

Jordan grinned. "Simple. We take the load as far as we have to, get it up to speed, aim it in the right direction, and let the whole thing go and come back for another load. Why waste watchmen on something you can't lose?"

The reporter had several questions and didn't know which one should be first.

Jordan said patiently, "All we do is aim it. Eventually it heads for something it shouldn't; then it kicks out of gear, if you want to use that phrase, weaves and gets back on course. All the time it's sending out a recognition signal. When it gets close to home someone is waiting for it, takes over, and lands it the same way it was shoved off. Think of a big slingshot at one end, and a fielder's glove on the other. OK?"

Surprisingly, the reporter came up with a question I hadn't thought of myself. "In other words, then, you don't really need a spaceship. You could travel in a glass fishbowl, if you wanted to."

Jordan eyed him with respect. "That's right, and it's been done. There are two reasons why not: traveling in space with nothing between you and the stars can drive you nuts. Pure, positive insanity. You have to have a den to creep into when you don't feel good. Would you like to walk over the Grand Canyon on a glass floor? Two, equipment *has* been known to break down. Spaceships like the KAYTA, and the landing ship you saw, have set after set of power source, set after set of navigational gear."

The reporter said, "What do you mean by 'power source'?" and when Jordan laughed happily he had the grace to turn red and apologize.

I said, pointing, "We've got company," as ahead of

us, at the head of our island, boats and cruisers were thronging. The reporter suddenly said, "Would it be all right if I got off here, Ken Jordan?"

His motive was plain; get to the Windsor *Star* with his story. We slowed almost to a stop, he pulled his towed Chriscraft close to jump from our stern, and as Jordan cast off the line his old diesel cranked up a clatter into a roar and off he went, swerving away to the Canadian shore and the nearest telephone, his pad of precious notes firmly clamped under his arm. Our own pilot yanked wide open the throttle of his turbines, skidded in a wide hovercraft turn, screamed down the Canadian shoreline into another glorious watery power slide, and zigzagged north into our own waters and our own entrance with our second hovercraft wailing at our heels. Our Russian pilots were breaking in some of our high schoolers as maintenance and steersmen, and I hoped our kids would be as good as their instructors.

The barges began to flow up the seaway from New Brunswick through the Welland Canal. As big as the *Tashmoo* had seemed to be when it took off, it was dwarfed by the giant aluminum frames over eight hundred feet long and ninety feet wide. They would have been bigger if the Welland locks had more capacity. Unseaworthy as they could be and almost impossible to tow against any kind of headwind, we lost at least two to a flash storm on Lake Erie in American waters. The State of New York thriftily salvaged them to use as breakwater fill for the proposed restoration of Niagara Falls; Jordan promptly presented New York with four more to help in the great engineering job. It took good timing to bring the barges together with the loads that were pouring in from all over the world and, since the seaway closed for the winter months, we had to stockpile barges in the summer and fall for winter loading by scuttling them in coveys in shallow Canadian waters, pumping them out when they were needed. The United States was in a pout because of our purchases from China and the Iron Curtain; the only winter routing left was east from Vancouver and Prince Rupert, west from Montreal. Both the Canadian Pacific and the Canadian National ran spurs down to the water's edge in southern Ontario, double-tracked everything that needed it through the Manitoba and Saskatchewan flatlands, and ran twin-quad diesels through the Canadian Rockies as a matter of course.

Belle River lot values skyrocketed when the railroad and loading crews moved in, and the tiny resort town became a showplace, another Cape Canaveral to watch our regular pickup and launching of the giant aluminum cargo carriers. Records are not clear, but provincial police, in friendly conversations with us, said that at least fourteen missing individuals were almost certain to have stowed away amid our cargoes. None of them, of course, were ever heard of again. There were many efforts to plant equipment in our barges and no doubt many of them succeeded. One box labeled furs, weighing and looking the same, was discovered by accident, and Jordan hired a technician to take it apart. When told it was a self-powered radio beacon, he just laughed and waved it away.

From time to time either Jordan or myself would stroll down to the entrance to pass the time of day with our Burns guards, asking light questions. It wasn't too hard, playing true or false, to discover which had sold out or was about to, and after that to arrange for a Burns substitute; I couldn't blame the bribe-takers, as the offers were tremendous to get into our island outpost just for a look. I say I can't blame them, either the bribe-takers or the bribe-givers, because it was open knowledge that our blocks of gold were casually stacked, blobs of resolidified gold lying on the grass where Jordan had showed the high schoolers how to use the oxygen lance to cut the blocks down to bandsaw-cutting size. And to see in the summer time the empty downbound freighters heave to in the steamer lane long enough to hoist millions of dollars' worth of gold aboard from the stern of our hovercraft certainly was enough to stir the ingenuity of any poverty-stricken hood.

The Royal Canadian Mounted kept us informed of everything they heard through the Canadian underworld, but we got no help from the FBI although the Michigan state police and the Detroit gendarmes came up with some excellent tips. Our turquoise-glowing shield was visible for miles from all angles, and so tempting as a target that anyone with a high-powered rifle was bound to try a few shots just to see if one would penetrate. None did, and Jordan never objected.

It was on a pleasant September evening that the first serious try was made.

By coincidence, Ken Jordan and myself were sitting near the rim of the high schoolers' swimming pool, watching the kids wear themselves out, and discussing the fact that the kids were getting restless. We had provided them with every luxury they wanted, and a few they had never thought of, but who want to be cooped up all the time? Each had a good bank account in Canada—gold!—and how about taking a vacation? We had made arrangements with the University of Chicago to supply instructors, and here it was fall and no one had had a vacation yet, forgetting they'd been on one for a long time, according to my working-stiff standards. Around the island, as always, were the groups of sightseeing small boats and cruisers, making broad and indecent guesses, no doubt, about what was going on inside.

We heard a roar above us, and we looked to see a plane diving directly into our roof access hole in the top of the dome. It was dusk, and the dome, with few openings, muffled outside sound, so the diving plane was almost on us before we knew it. No one even had time to scream. We found out later it was a Beechcraft twin-engine. The pilot had dived directly at our dome's opening, locked the controls, and bailed out when he was certain he was aimed right and the wings were about to peel off. The plane, crammed with aviation gas and explosive, crashed exactly where it was aimed. The cabin, loaded with extra fuel, flared into flame and the contact-fused explosive blew the fire in all directions, dripping down the wall of our dome in horrid crimson gobs and putting an ugly red glow on everything.

At the same time, the cruisers threw off their sightseeing pretense, opened their engines, and hit our tunnel entrance. The assailants, army-surplus helmeted, were armed with machine guns and grenades, and the first cruiser in our entrance tunnel poured out bazooka crews who jumped out in the shallows when their cruiser grounded and began pumping shells down the tunnel into our island at random.

The aerial projectile, however, hitting our roof opening dead center, failed to penetrate through the Regan shield. It hung there, and it was an eerie sight to see death and flames almost directly over your head, harmless. The kids were screaming, shouting, and when the flaming plane, wings bent like a dying angel, began to slide down the sides of the dome carrying its burning gas tanks with it, it was almost a genuine panic.

"Shut up," Jordan roared. He bellowed other things and the high schoolers began to quiet down. Just then the tunnel raid began, and the panic started all over again. Jordan snarled something vicious, and trotted away toward the entrance, me after him with my heart in my throat. The unarmed Burns guards ran past us as we hurried, heading for the dubious safety of our palms. When we got to the entrance the bazooka shells were bursting halfway down the tunnel, just short of our island ground. Jordan pulled up short, me with him. He was breathing hard. "Bastards!" he snarled. "Bastards! I'll fix 'em." He walked directly into the tunnel, facing the impotent fire, made a gesture I've never seen outside of Naples, spun around, and came back to dart inside our office building and out again. We stood there together, me shuddering and shaking although I knew we were safe, Jordan with his face changed into a hateful mask, the bazooka shells slamming and blasting almost in our faces.

Then the whole section of the dome flared outward.

The bazooka crews, the machine gunners, the cruisers, the houseboat with a crane and a small bulldozer on the deck, the men splashing through the shallows to invade us, they all melted. Not in a flash, not in a flare, and not so quickly that we couldn't see the tanks of the boats explode, the men fall in the water and roll to try to put out the fire that was eating their bodies, the fire that even consumed the water. Probably they screamed. We heard nothing inside our outpost. I got sick to my stomach and vomited. I ran for the bushes, then for my office, the sight of the melting mass too bright in my mind to tolerate. When I came out, everything was dark. Jordan was standing in the same spot, staring at nothing. I went up to him. I put my arms around him. His body was tense as music wire. Then he softened, he put his arms around me, and we fell down on the grass together.

## Chapter Nineteen

In the morning I lay there for a while listening to the sparrows chirp. Maybe I'd pick us up some songbirds, I thought, if I knew what kind to ask for. When I opened my eyes, Ken Jordan was standing by my window, his face in shadow, looking at me.

"Well, hi," he said.

"Hi," and I wiggled my toes under the sheet. There was a pause.

"I suppose," he said finally, "this is one of the mornings when you hate yourself."

"Should I?"

"Well, do you?"

"This is no time for psychology," I told him. "There's a bathroom I want to use. Go find the coffeepot and put something in it."

When he was gone I scooted across the hall. I looked in the mirror much longer than I usually did. When I got to the kitchen he had the toaster going and was putting eggs in a bubbling saucepan. I said "I like my eggs fried and basted, not boiled."

He dunked the last in the water. "Boiled eggs are good for you. And no frying pan to wash."

When the eggs were eaten, the second cup of

coffee poured, and the cigarettes lit, he leaned back with his eyes on me.

"Well, do you?" he went on, taking up the conversation where he'd left off.

I was never the coy type. I said "No."

The corners of his mouth went up. "Was it good?"

I flared at him. "What the hell do you want—testimonials?" I had to grin at the expression on his face. "Yes, it was good." Then I remembered.

Quickly, with concern, "What's the matter?"

It took me a minute to sort things out. "I'm not really sure. I don't think I want to be sure." I leaned on the table and my eyes met his. "I'm no angel. But I'm no devil either. What possessed me to throw myself at you, with all those dying men just a few feet from me? And what made you throw yourself back at me?"

He winced. "I don't know," and the words dragged out. "Lee's thoughts said *no*! so hard I got sick inside. My own idea was to kill, kill, kill, so no one would ever try it again. Do you know what would have happened if we hadn't had a field around that dome? That plane would have blown everyone apart. No, I did what I wanted to do at the time. And I'm not a bit sorry. Sick, maybe, but not sorry . . . And then you came along at just that moment, soft and warm and shaking all over. You know, kid, that's the first time you looked soft and warm since you finagled your way into my room at the hotel; usually you look and act like you're made of 8-10 stainless. You look soft and warm right now, come to think about it."

Without warning the big jerk got up far enough to smack me a big eggy, toasty kiss, and without warning I blushed redder than I've done since high school. When he lurched back clumsily into his chair and looked embarrassment at me, we both began to smile self-consciously, laugh together, and ended up holding hands across the table.

Finally he stood up and reminded me it was time to go to work. "You'll have thousands of calls as soon as you open up the switchboard," he said. "No comment, as far as you're concerned. We just repelled an invasion of our territory, if that's the phrase. I'll have to pick out some of the older kids with strong stomachs and get that mess cleaned out," and his face clouded over as he remembered the grisly flame he had caused.

I left the dishes on the sink and we went out the kitchen door together. I went out first, stopped so suddenly he bumped into me. "Oh, no!" I said faintly.

Seated in a solemn semicircle on the grass were all my high schoolers. As he stepped out after me blinking at the soft morning light the two of us stood there in front of the juvenile jury. When each of the young devils nodded his or her head in knowing unison, and came out with a rehearsed "uh-huh," my face turned brick red. Getting caught in the act can be embarrassing; the chaperone never should. I looked up at Ken, who was grinning from ear to ear. The kids just sat there, uh-huhing.

"All right," I squeaked. I took a deep breath and started again. "All right; we've had our fun. Now it's time to go to work." Instantly, they all howled, and I realized, too late, what I'd said. They broke up their tombstone semicircle and scattered as Ken and I walked down to the office. When we walked past the entrance the bazooka teams had tried to force, I turned my head away. Ken hesitated and then, muttering something about a firehose, left me. I went into the office, glared at the two smirking girls on the switchboard, and began to answer the calls that jammed our lines.

All in all, twenty-seven bodies were picked up down the Detroit River all the way to Amherstburg and all carrying records as long as your arm; how many assailants there were never became accurately known. Ken washed out the remains in our tunnel entrance with a firehose; the metal frames and engines of the attacking cruisers stayed there for a long time until some daring salvagers sneaked into our waters much later and hauled them away. No attempts at robbery or invasion were ever made again.

The plane crash on our dome, and the flare, had of course been seen from both American and Canadian shores. Following Ken's orders, I merely said we had been defending ourselves and let it go at that; this was not enough for the frantically curious press, and it was not too long before we were regarded as no better than murderers. This despite the fact at least twenty-seven unsuccessful hoods had tried their very level best to wipe us out. No one ever quite got around to saying we should have been wiped out, but the feeling was there.

By winter time, when the seaway closed, we had enough barges stockpiled along the Canadian shore to take care of the trainloads that poured in from the east and west coasts. The lake ice was at first a problem, but with the scuttled barges pumped out it was not hard to haul the awkward monsters close enough to shore to load right from the waterfront. It got so that when the spaceship came down to pick up another barge it drew no more interest from the working crews than a passing jetliner.

In our dome the weather was comfortable, the greenhouse effect making our climate almost tropical despite ice on the river. The turquoise color changed from day to day, depending on how much of the infrared and ultraviolet was needed to maintain our temperature. Mac, my old government boss, called me several times. To my surprise he had not been fired. If anything, he now had an even more important job, in charge of a much larger crew. He tried to get invited to our island. "No," I told him. "Nothing in common anymore."

"How about dinner someplace?"

"Thanks," I said. "I'm allergic to questions. Besides, if you spirited me away on your knightly charger, Ken Jordan would come and get me. And don't think he couldn't, either."

Mac tried other tactics, none of which worked. Although I told him over and over I had switched sides because I wanted to, and not under duress, he found it hard to believe. He used patriotism, he tried threats (which I laughed at), he tried rewards, offers of promotion—finally I got bored and told the girls I would no longer accept calls from him.

One thing led to another, and I finally had to face the fact that the United States of America was developing a definite antagonism toward us. And for the Canadian government, which the American public thought, was protecting us. As if we needed any protection! Some, naturally, was due to the savage Fundamentalist strain that lies deep in so many Americans; the youngsters we were shielding, our refusal to send the kids back to their parents. Actually, as time passed, the young ones grew further and further away from their parents, their homes. What would they go back to—stealing hubcaps, paper routes, shoplifting? Under our dome they were working, learning, having fun, earning more in a month than their parents did in a year. Every bit of equipment, including our switchboard and wiring, was being operated and maintained by boys and girls in their teens. They mowed the lawn, cooked and served the meals, ordered and stocked toilet paper and teaspoons, piloted and repaired the hovercrafts, and at least six of them were competent pilots and navigators of our one jet airliner. What youngster, doing a man's job, wanted to go back to the Michigan or Canadian mainland where they had to observe curfews, where they could not drink legally, where they could not vote and yet were drafted for military service? When any of them left the island, it was only to Canada (and our Canadian youngsters were very careful they had a Regan passport). Their parents could visit the island if they wished, but the visits grew shorter and further apart as the months went by.

And as the months went by, there were eleven more marriages. The Americans did not like that. Not with two of them being interracial.

Some of the American dislike was certainly wounded pride, and a lot of it was wounded Detroit pride. The Motor City, the Arsenal of Democracy in Two World Wars, or some such catchword, sat grimly and watched while freighter after freighter, loaded with goods from all parts of the world, sailed smugly past the city. Radio, television, magazines, and newspapers sniped and pounded, fretted and nagged, and with the peculiarities of style and construction that meant there was a central source. Ken had given up appearing at the United Nations. "Wouldn't they like to catch me on American soil?" he said bitterly. "Especially after the American ambassador walked out the last time I showed up?"

When I mentioned he had a spaceship to use, he gently reminded me that Lee Lukkari was studying on the cruiser KAYTA, unavailable, and the landing craft hauling off our barges was on automatic pilot. For the first time it occurred to me that I had never asked where the KAYTA was. He chuckled softly.

"Same place as Earth. On the other side of the sun."

"Why?" I asked. "Isn't that rather inconvenient?"

"Think back," he said. "How big is it?"

I thought back to my orientation, to the *Tashmoo* taking off and the feeling I had had when the *Tashmoo* went straight up. "I never thought about that," I admitted. "It would give a lot of people an inferiority complex."

The United States, happily enough, was pulling out of its financial depression. The gold we were pouring to the overseas nations was trickling back through North America as the wealth seeped down from the top. Some Asiatic and some South American countries were now able to supply a living diet for almost everyone; the next step after necessities and comforts was luxuries, and those the United States could supply in almost any degree. Little by little factories begun to open, making new or retooled or restyled products, and although the big portion of the national income was still going to the war establishment, the unemployment rate began to go down and ads for help wanted started to show in the American newspapers. Did we get any credit? Of course not.

Surface politeness was still the rule for international behavior, but tempers were getting shorter every day if one read between the lines of the newspapers and magazines. One United States senator spoke at length on the thesis that what his country needed to pull out of its slump was a good war. Not a big war, just a small neat war that would use up some of the stockpiled munitions. After all, the United States was paying for a three-million-man army, wasn't it?

Perhaps another nice quiet little foreign war might

have been the answer. As it was, just before the American presidential elections, with taxes at a new high, the great cities leaking people to the suburbs and needing transfusions of billions of dollars merely to stay alive, crime rates astronomical, and actual hunger in more than one American area, America's last war started at home.

It began on Detroit's East Side, with a steady driving west wind.

## Chapter Twenty

Somewhere east of shabby, rundown—but still lily-white—Indian Village, a fire started. Or perhaps it was set. The area, as I remember it, was almost solidly frame two-family houses, each on thirty-foot lots with narrow 1920 walkways between, and with wood-shingled roofs. By the time firemen arrived the flames had spread to houses on either side. One burning brand was carried across the street by the west wind to land on a bone-dry shingle.

In minutes the whole block was ablaze, and the firemen retreated, fighting every step of the way. Every East Side fire rig hit the streets in the next hour, the West Side rigs following in their turn. This was on Thursday.

By Friday the sky was black, the Canadian shores lined with awed sightseers watching half a city die.

The fire spread on all sides, back west, hurdling in turn Kercheval and Vernor and Mack and Warren, sent flaming darts across Jefferson, racing ahead of itself to the Grosse Pointes and dying sullenly at Pemberton, but north of Jefferson eating its way out to Balfour. Finally the west wind died, and the fire crews who came from all over Michigan held it at the

Eaton plant and the Detroit City Airport. When it was all over, Detroit was ashes from the river and Grosse Pointe to Gratiot to the downtown business area. At least four thousand bodies were buried, most of them unidentified and almost all of them Negro.

The homeless fled. Some to Harper Woods, some to Warren, some to Pontiac and Rochester, some to Livonia and Southfield, some to Gibraltar and Trenton, all of them panicky, hungry, tired, angry, and ugly. At least half a million people, most of them Negro.

In the ensuing riots, which were triggered by desperation and shock than by hatred, some eight hundred were killed by the Eighty-second Airborne called in from Kentucky. Units of the Michigan National Guard, at the very last, were fighting each other along color lines. The United States government declared Detroit a disaster area, and supplies began to flow in. But it was too late.

In Cambodia, the spearheading Seventh Division, 75 percent Negro, laid down its arms and flatly refused to fight when the fire casualty totals and ratios got overseas. The Chinese-backed Cambodians probed the suddenly silent American lines, found the vacuum and captured enough prisoners to explain the surprising inaction, and Peking flipped a coin in a wild, insane toss. Fourteen Chinese divisions, sixty more in reserve or on the way, smashed the American lines. Everything American collapsed in Cambodia, and in Asia.

Even during the worst of the foreign debacle, the military retained its discipline. At least four hundred of the mutinous Seventh Division were drumhead courtmartialed and executed, some of them even as the Chinese were pouring over the parade ground.

The newly elected President of the United States,

fresh from an inspection trip of the ruins of Detroit on the way to a television appearance to plead for national unity, was assassinated by a uniformed Negro on leave from the Seventh Division.

The entire South Side of Chicago went up in flames on a windless day. At least forty separate fires were set.

Los Angeles burned. Baltimore. Newark. Memphis. A third of New York City. Half of Cleveland, a quarter of Toledo. All of Scranton, all of Pittsburgh except the Golden Triangle. Part of Washington. Jacksonville, Talladega, Tupelo. Little Rock, Brownsville, Paducah, Cincinnati, Milwaukee.

Ken and I sat quietly in our little German-style bar, listening to the reports and watching the havoc on the screen. In the background our music box was tinkling, "Wien, Wien, nur du allein."

"It's spreading over here, too," I said.

Ken looked at me questioningly.

"One of our girls. She got stoned, name-calling, in downtown Windsor. Her family's lived in Blenheim since 1859, but she's Negro."

"Yeah."

"Ken," I said, "how long is this going to go on?"

"I'm not God," was all he would say.

Late that night the United States Army took the new President into protective custody; the next day the United States Senate and the House of Representatives voted, under the guns of Eighty-second Airborne white troops, full charge of the economy to one General Purdy Calhoun for the duration of the national emergency. On television that night, General Calhoun ordered national cooperation, national unity, and full wartime mobilization. The United States Sixth Fleet was ordered out of the Mediterranean to the Far East via the Panama Canal. All SAC aircraft were ordered into the air. The Minutemen complexes throughout the country were alerted. General Calhoun also ordered the Chinese troops out of Cambodia back to a hundred miles north of the China-Cambodian border. *Ordered* them!

The first Chinese missile hit Bremerton Naval Base just fourteen minutes before four Poseidon submarine-based missiles eliminated Peking. Despite saturation-fire and elaborate countermissile tactics by both sides, bases in the United States and in the Chinese hinterlands continued to operate until every major Chinese and American city was eliminated. The American West Coast, together with the islands of Japan, fell completely out of contact and in many areas under water as subterranean volcanic action began. In the United States, Washington as the first target and New York as the second preceded Pittsburgh, Cleveland, and Chicago. Two Chinese missiles, certainly aimed at Detroit, detonated in Lake Ste. Clair, and drifting radioactivity contaminated the Midwest to Minnesota under the prevailing winds.

That was the first wave.

There was no third.

The second wave of missiles was sporadic and almost unaimed in its randomness. Some landed in Pensacola and Bangor, some in Angkor Thom and the delta of the Yalu. No longrange Chinese bombers ever reached the American mainland, although Mauna Loa, with its entire top blown off, was stimulated into violent eruption; a single SAC bomber returned to its Fairbanks base, killing its crew in crashlanding. Other malfunctioning missiles eliminated Ottawa, Waltham, and South Bend. Pompeii was forever eliminated as an archaeological site, Albuquerque as a railroad division change, Leeds and Birmingham and Sheffield as manufacturing centers.

Europe and the British Isles lost three million population; Russia and the Balkans, eight million; Asia Minor, including Turkey, only a few hundred thousand; Mexico, six million, all of whom were of the Mexican Federal District; and South and Central America went untouched, if one excepts the opening of the Panama Canal as a sea-level gap in the continental chain. United States casualties were uncertain, and based only upon the cessation of radio and television contact from different areas can it be guessed at a hundred and forty million deaths. Chinese casualties were close to one hundred percent including Korea and areas down to the Indian Ocean. The last operative American missile bases continued to throw their bombs at least a day after the last Chinese missile was fired. It landed in Detroit.

I saw it hit.

I happened to be walking from our office building to my own apartment, nerves wound tight from the news we had been hearing on the air and from the taut atmosphere. Through the turquoise shell of our dome I could see the spire of the Penobscot Tower to downriver right, illuminated by the rays of the sinking smoky red sun. Then there was a giant flare behind the Penobscot Building and it flew to pieces. The fireball jumped to giant size, taking in the whole world before our dome went black. The ground quivered and shook, and I had the strange delusion that the dome itself was gritting its teeth, hunching its shoulders, digging in.

Everyone poured out of our office building and apartments, white-faced and shuddery, the two babies crying. There was no panic; Ken Jordan was there, grim and worried. The dome was still ebony-black, our only lights fading and flickering until they went off completely, leaving us in blackness. Then our power source took over, and the lights came on again. Ken came directly to me.

I said "Detroit," shakily, pointed to the direction where the missile had hit. He nodded sadly, shortly turned on his heel and started back to his own office, disregarding the youngsters that tried to question him on his way. I spent a bad two hours getting everyone quieted down enough to go to their own apartments and to bed. Before it was time for dawn I was on the west end of the island, waiting for the sun. Ken was already there. Maybe he had been there all night.

The dome was now almost greenish, a light green through which we could see both American and Canadian shorelines. Just downriver from us was one of our aluminum barges, drifting silently away. There was nothing else.

Detroit and Windsor were flat. Oh, here and there bulked up a pile of rubble, a thread of smoke, or a wisp of fire. As far as we could see there was nothing. Silently Ken and I stood up and walked back to our tunnel entrance. On Riverside Drive our hovercraft dock was smashed, there was no traffic on the drive, the Walker Distillery was gone. The great pile of coal at the Ford plant was gone, and the tall stack of the Ford powerhouse. We walked across the island, and Detroit Edison's Seven Sisters were no longer standing at the foot of Lycaste.

Ken said finally, "An hour for breakfast, no more. Then get everybody out here; I want to talk to them."

"All right," I said, and I began to cry without tears.

There were forty-six boys. There were forty-nine girls, and two babies. It took longer than an hour, because each of them had to inspect the desolation visible through our dome as Ken and I had done. It was closer to three hours before everyone was sitting in a group in front of us.

Ken's face was drawn. He said abruptly, "You've all seen what's left out there. All of you had friends out there, most of you had parents and relatives. They're all gone." Heavily: "All gone."

One girl started crying, then another, and soon all but the two mothers of the tiny babies were sobbing. Ken seemed unmoved. He went on, stonily.

"There's no American radio or TV on the air. Radio London says India is invading Pakistan; Russia and Germany are invading France; Holland and Belgium are flooded. Face it. This is the end."

The sobbing broke out again.

"I'm leaving," he said. "Dana Iverson is leaving. I'm supposed to leave you here. Oh, you'd be safe from bombs, from radioactivity, from anything. I'm supposed to leave you here in a world without a future, leave you here to starve to death when your food runs out." It was quiet except for a baby's giggle. "I can't do it. I'm going to take you with me if you want to come."

"No," he went on, "I can't take you as citizens of the Regan Group. I can take you as baggage, as immigrants. I can take you as second-class fodder. If you want Regan citizenship you'll have to earn it, and it won't be easy. If you leave with us, you'll leave naked, penniless, homeless; you'll take your chances as they come." He hesitated. "I won't even ask you if you want to become citizens at a later date. This doesn't apply to the parents of the two babies. As parents of a Regan citizen, they will occupy a sort of a special honored position, and will be treated that way. The rest of you will have to earn position or honors. You have a few minutes to think it over," and he turned abruptly to me. "Coming?" And he walked away.

We sat for the last time in an Earth bar. It was deathly quiet. I said, "I'm glad, Ken. I'm glad you decided to take them along. Even if it's never been done before."

"Yeah," he said. "Well, I *had* to," he burst out.

"I know it," I said, "and I'm glad. If even one wants to stay, I stay, too."

"I figured that. That might have had something to do with it."

"Thanks," I said. "Thanks. I hope it did. Especially because I'm pregnant."

"What?" unbelievingly.

"At least a month," I admitted. "Get out of the habit of taking pills, and make one mistake . . . bingo."

"Bingo," he said in wonder. "Bingo!"

"Sit right there," I warned him. "This is no time to get romantic."

"Yes," he said, resting back in his chair. "No time to get romantic, God knows . . ."

"You take this pretty casually," I said.

"Casually? Well, what the hell—say, you take this pretty easy yourself!"

I shrugged. "I've had a month or so to think it over."

"Well?"

"Well, the father isn't so bad."

"Do you like the father?"

"Sure," I said. "Ever since he got off the booze and began acting like a human being."

"You like him, but you don't love him."

"I wouldn't go so far as to say that."

"Well, damn it," he said, "do you or don't you?"

"Hah," I said cagily. "You first."

"All right," he snarled. "So I love you. What do you know about that?"

"OK," I said. "That makes twice. So I love you. What do you know about that?"

"Twice?"

"The first time was the night I got pregnant. Of course," I said helpfully, "I can understand you forgetting it. Your attention was being distracted at the time. Get away from me, you rapist," but he didn't, not right away.

Not too much later, the KAYTA appeared overhead. I remembered the *Tashmoo* going up and mentally compared the KAYTA for size, and smiled wistfully at my naïveté. Even miles up, the KAYTA was enormous. The smaller ship came down through the center of the dome. Lee Lukkari got out. She took one look at Ken with his arm around me and knew. Give her credit: she smiled.

She was not surprised at Ken's demand to take all the kids along. "This I expected," matter-of-factly, and counted heads. "Two trips," she said. "Everyone knows the terms? Everyone?" and she went from face to face. What she saw satisfied her. "All right," she announced.

There was a pause and one of the girls said, "Can't I take—"

Lee Lukkari's head, Ken's, and mine all swiveled together. No.

Another hesitation, and then the first boy started up the ramp, hand in hand with a girl. Already they were pairing off. Then another, and another two, until more than half had disappeared into the ship. Lee Lukkari said shortly, "Next trip," walked up the ramp, and the ship took off. No one said much until she came down again.

Ken and I were the last to enter. Lee Lukkari

waited at the top of the ramp while we walked up. We stood together at the entrance, looking at the scattered fires still burning in the ruins of Windsor and Detroit. One of our barges was idling in shoal water on the American side, square nose down in the shallows. Ken looked at me, and I looked at him. There was nothing to say. We turned, walked into the ship, and the ramp swung up, and that was all. That was a long time ago.

To tell a story, you begin at the beginning and go on until the end.

# EPILOGUE

My grandmothers must have been remarkable women, especially Dana Iverson. She and my grandad Ken died almost at the same time; grandmother Lee deliberately (I feel quite sure), quietly ceased to live not long later.

Grandmother Dana's radical attitudes never ceased to startle, shock, and please her friends. Until my admission rites when I became a woman, when I became entitled to full information in the Archives, I even felt embarrassed to live in the only family with two grandmothers and one grandfather. Now, of course, I am proud to have ancestors like them in my bloodline. If I ever have a child I'll try to see he is proud, too.

As grandmother Dana grew old, she spent much time talking about the planet she came from. The Archives indicate there is a good chance life might have survived, and rebuilt. I hope so. Even their dome might still be in existence. I hope so.

Some day, if my career goes well, I will command a Regan cruiser of my own. I hope so.

If I do, I will try to at least tread the ground where my grandfather and my grandmothers once walked. If I do, it will give me great pleasure.

I know so.